# Catching the Light

Mary Grand

First published in the United Kingdom and worldwide 2016

ISBN 978-1523453191

Printed by CreateSpace

## Dedication

'Catching the Light' is dedicated to all my lovely cocker spaniel-owning friends at Cockers Online and Cockers on Facebook

## Acknowledgements

Many thanks to Andrew, Lucy and Adele for all their help and support with reading and commenting on these stories before publication. Thanks to Pixabay for the cover image.

# Contents

Page

1     The New Arrival

24    Catching the Light

40    Belonging

64    The Outing

89    Free to Be Tegan (extract)

114    About the Author

# The New Arrival

**"Every once in a while a dog enters your life and changes everything." Anonymous**

Rachel froze. Who was it? Since she moved here a month ago she had kept her distance, and developed a cold polite smile that was as effective as an electric fence. People kept away.

Reluctantly, she went to the door, glad it was still light at half past nine on an August evening. She peered through the glass and saw her neighbour. What did she want?

Slowly she opened the door, but held it ajar. Both women were about fifty, but their appearance was very different. Rachel, determined to become invisible, wore no make up, had cut her shoulder length brown hair short and hid her trim figure under a baggy shirt dress. Sarah simply wore again the skirt and t shirt that she had flung over the chair the night before and had yet to brush her hair.

'I'm so sorry to bother you-' Sarah said.

'It's OK-' Rachel tried to sound politely busy.

'It's a bit complicated.' Rachel saw Sarah gaze over her shoulder, inviting herself in, and so reluctantly opened the door. Sarah came straight in.

'It's about Olive. You know, the neighbour the other side of me. She's had a fall. The ambulance has just taken her to hospital. I've rung her daughter Fiona. She's on her way over now, but you know what the ferries are like in August.'

Rachel did and, unlike most inhabitants of the Isle of Wight, she relished being cut off from 'the mainland.' The Solent was her moat. It was why she had decided her to escape here.

'The problem is Lottie.'

'Lottie?'

'Well, Olive is terribly worried about her. I said I'd sort something out. You see, her Fiona is allergic.'

Rachel wondered if Sarah had been drinking.

'Sorry?'

'Oh, silly me. Lottie is Olive's dog. You must have seen her: pretty little black cocker spaniel. Mind you, what Olive's son thought he was doing getting his mother a dog last Christmas, I don't know. Crazy with her health problems; and where is he now? Scarpered off to live in Australia.'

Rachel was wondering if Sarah was ever going to get to the point.

'I've been ringing round,' continued Sarah, 'you know, kennels and places. All fine for next week when the schools have gone back, but booked up solid this week.'

Rachel was starting to have an inkling about where the conversation was heading.

'So you will be taking in Lottie in?' she asked.

'The thing is, she's a darling, but terrible with cats. You know, I have three.'

'Yes, they come in my garden.'

'Lottie just chases them, and Tinker, well, she's expecting kittens any day now.'

'More cats?'

'Oh, they've all got good homes waiting for them. I'll have her done then. The thing is, I was wondering if you could possibly take Lottie in, just until the weekend.'

Rachel shook her head so hard her neck cricked.

'No, definitely not. There must be someone else, another dog owner-'

'But there really isn't anyone. Everyone is either away, or I have no number for them. You are here on your own, aren't you?'

Rachel instinctively became evasive. 'At the moment-'

'Well?'

'But I've never owned a dog-'

Sarah smiled broadly. 'It's OK. The main thing is that you will be around her. She hates being left on her own for long.'

'She sounds very needy.'

'Oh, just a cocker spaniel, you know.'

Rachel didn't know.

'Do you have anything on this week?' persisted Sarah.

Rachel looked down. It was the end of summer, posters on shop windows shouted 'Back to School.' She should be anticipating a new class of children (and their parents), going into an empty classroom to prepare. However, for the first time in twenty five years, she had no class waiting for her. It hurt; she felt bereft.

'No, I suppose I don't,' she said quietly.

Sarah pounced on the first sign of weakness. 'There we are then. Lottie is toilet trained, the lot. Lively, but as good as gold. I'll go through her routine with you. We should go and get her. She's looking so confused, poor thing.'

'This minute?'

'Oh, yes. Come on.'

Rachel looked around at her pristine home, free of dog hair, dog smells and muddy paw prints. Could she face it all? She was aware of Sarah waiting and then thought of the poor old lady, maybe she should help.

'I suppose for a few nights-' she said.

'Great, I've got the keys.' Sarah headed out of the door. Rachel grabbed her own keys. They went into Olive's bungalow and were greeted enthusiastically by Lottie, who came running to them. She was so excited, jumping up and running around in circles. Rachel moved back, but Sarah leant down and stroked her. 'Ah, poor thing. You must be wondering where your mum has gone.'

Rachel cringed. She never understood this mum and dad thing with pet owners.

Sarah handed her a large bag, dog bed, and blanket, and put Lottie on her lead.

They went back to Rachel's house and into the kitchen.

'Well, this is very tidy,' Sarah commented.

It was true, but even Rachel had to admit it was clinically tidy: not like home at all.

Sarah went through Lottie's routine. It seemed pretty straightforward until it came to the walks.

'Olive sometimes pays a young girl Molly to walk her in the morning, up to the castle. I think there's a group up there, meet about eight o'clock at the car park by the moat. Obviously, they don't go inside. All very informal, but Lottie has friends there.'

'Lottie has friends?' Rachel smiled. Really, that was a bit ridiculous.

'Oh, yes. It might be a good idea to keep her in routine. They're a nice group from the sound of it. I know Alex who goes. She writes for our local paper, ever so friendly.'

'A journalist?' Rachel turned pale.

Sarah didn't notice. 'That's right. Anyway, look out for them all.'

Rachel nodded, but had no intention of meeting up. Meanwhile, Lottie seemed to be making herself at home. She was nosing in cupboards. Rachel followed, shutting them tightly. Lottie was busily sniffing around the floor, then went to the back door. She sat there patiently. Rachel watched. Lottie looked back at her, then lifted a paw and scratched the door.

'She's asking to go out to pee. What a good girl,' said Sarah enthusiastically.

'On the lawn?'

'I'm afraid you'll have a few yellow patches now. In here's Olive's dog walking bag, and, you know, poo bags and things.'

Rachel panicked: why hadn't she thought of that? Oh God, not dog poo! Sarah, however, seemed oblivious of her disgust.

'There are bins up at the castle. Let me show you how to pick up using the poo bag.'

Rachel watched horrified, mentally adding disposable gloves and hand wash.

'Right, I must get back. Joe's on shifts, need to pack his dinner. You know what these men are, helpless.'

Sarah left, and Rachel heard Lottie scratch at the door again. Rushing to save the paintwork, she let her out. She watched flabbergasted as Lottie went tearing around the garden, checking out the fences (fortunately secure). A pigeon landed on the garden and Lottie went charging towards it; the bird easily flew away. Then Rachel saw Sarah's large tabby sitting on the top of the fence. Lottie barked at him, but the cat just sat washing his paws. Lottie looked back at Rachel for help. 'You can't reach him,' she said. Lottie barked again, but gave in and went to sniff around the pots. To Rachel's horror she peed against her best Portmeirion plant holder. Sarah went to fill up a bucket of water to wash it off, and Lottie joined her, drinking the water coming out of the tap.

Lottie went back into the house. Rachel followed her, hoping Lottie would stay in the kitchen on her bed. She turned on the TV and restarted the Lewis DVD she had been watching. Quietly, Lottie came in, put her head on Rachel's knees, and looked up longingly.

'No way. Not on my white leather sofa.'

Lottie sighed and cuddled up on top of Rachel's feet. Rachel felt guilty; poor Lottie must be confused. She climbed down from the sofa and on to the floor. Lottie climbed straight onto her lap, her head planted firmly on her chest. Rachel stroked her head and her ears, long and soft. Lottie looked up at her adoringly.

'You don't care. You don't judge me, do you?' Rachel said, stroking her.

Rachel found comfort in the warmth of Lottie's body. It felt a long time since anyone had cuddled her. When the DVD finished, Rachel eased Lottie off her. It was bed time. She guessed she should take Lottie out to the garden. Normally, she would have just locked the back door. It was strange to be outside on a summer's evening. Rachel breathed in the scent of the delicate white flowers on the star jasmine and looked up at the sky. She saw what at first she thought was a bird, then realised it was a bat, and beyond that, in the sky, she saw thousands of stars. Lottie, she realised, was doing her circuit, running the perimeter of the garden, which she followed with a quick pee on the Portmeirion pot. Rachel, suddenly tired, decided to wash it off tomorrow. They went inside.

'Now,' she said to Lottie, 'This is your bed. You settle down and I'll see you in the morning.' She felt silly talking to a dog, but Lottie was watching her. She looked rather sad, but then Rachel thought that maybe with those eyes she always would. She hardened her heart and went upstairs.

7

As she changed into her nightie, a face appeared around the bedroom door.

'Hey, downstairs.' She took Lottie back down and closed the kitchen door.

'Hoooo, hoooo,' she heard. What was she meant to do? The noise was so sad. She went back down. Lottie was sitting up on her bed looking even sadder. 'You must be confused, I suppose,' Rachel said. 'Strange house, all alone.' Lottie continued looking at her longingly.

'Well, just tonight.' Rachel carried the dog bed upstairs, closely followed by Lottie. She lay the bed down next to her own bed. Lottie climbed on, gave a contented sigh, and went to sleep. Rachel turned off the light. She could hear the gentle breathing of Lottie next to her, and soon she was asleep.

The next morning Rachel was woken at seven by a lick on her cheek. Startled, she sat up, and reminded herself about Lottie. They went downstairs together. Lottie went straight to the back door. Rachel let her out and put the kettle on. Soon Lottie returned, and watched Rachel while she ate her breakfast, followed her upstairs, waited while she showered, then trotted after her into the bedroom, and waited again while she dressed. 'You really don't like being on your own, do you?' Rachel said to Lottie. 'Time for a walk before your breakfast.'

Lottie started to run around in excited circles. Rachel struggled to attach the lead to Lottie's collar, picked up the dog bag, and left.

It was a beautiful morning. Lottie pulled her along enthusiastically. Rachel decided Lottie needed to run. She would take her up to the fields behind the castle. It would be alright; no one knew her.

Rachel walked down the lane, past bushes ripe with blackberries. There were some yellowing leaves in the trees, reminding her that autumn was on its way. Rachel liked this term. Harvest ran smoothly into Christmas, busy and purposeful. She sighed. They crossed the bridge over the ford. She let Lottie have a drink from the stream, but kept her on the lead. In the field there were sheep nibbling the cress that grew at the edge of the stream. She took out her mobile and took photos ready for later.

Rachel saw the sign post pointing up a steep hill to Carisbrooke Castle and followed it. Once at the top she breathed in the wonderful sight of the castle. The sun warmed the stone walls and cast a mellow glow. She heard a screeching of crows and realised they were seeing off an enormous buzzard. There was a number of dogs up there, most off lead. She felt uneasy, but the dogs were not interested in her: they all wanted to greet Lottie. Fortunately, Lottie was not too bothered and carried on sniffing the ground intently. Suddenly, a woman approached and said, 'Hi Lottie, where's Molly this morning?'

Rachel guessed she was meant to reply. 'I am looking after Lottie. Olive had a fall. She's in hospital.'

Suddenly, people who had all seemed preoccupied with their dogs started asking her about

Olive. They seemed to know a lot about her and her family.

'Don't suppose that useless son of hers will be over from Australia,' said a rather severe older man, wearing scruffy jeans and a checked shirt.

'Typical man,' said a young woman with a pushchair.

A smart older woman seemed to notice Rachel. 'I'm Eleanor, lovely to meet you.' Rachel took in the styled thick white hair, black cropped trousers, white t shirt and light beige gilet.

Disarmed by Eleanor's friendliness, Rachel introduced herself.

The younger girl looked up from sorting out her toddler. 'I'm Tania. That scruff over there is Dipsy.' She pointed out a large curly haired dog bounding down the moat. She's a labradoodle, crazy.'

'You can let Lottie off. Her recall is very good,' said Eleanor.

'Oh, I don't know-'

'Really, she never goes far.'

Lottie was looking very restless. Nervously, Rachel let her off. She panicked as Lottie went running after the labradoodle, but, after a brief greeting, Lottie went back to sniffing the grass. She was completely engrossed, only occasionally looking up.

'Oh God, there's a bloody horse,' said the scruffy man.

'David, for God's sake, put Phoebe on the lead' said Eleanor. She turned to Rachel, smiling. 'Lottie will be fine; horses don't freak her. Phoebe, though, hates them.'

Rachel watched as David put a very docile looking Dalmatian on a lead. 'David is a GP,' explained Eleanor. 'He likes being grumpy up here. I think it's a reaction to having to be polite to his patients the rest of the time.'

'Bloody sue me if I so much as scowl nowadays,' said David. Rachel saw however that he was grinning.

'Where are your dogs?' Rachel asked Eleanor.

'They're in the hedges. Hope they haven't killed a rabbit. You know, they had a half each once, wouldn't drop it until we got home.'

Rachel tried to laugh, but the picture was so horrific she couldn't.

She found herself walking around with the group. Without really meaning to, she realised she had told them that she used to be a teacher, and had been on the island for a month. Rachel in her turn learnt that Tania was in the middle of a row with her toddler's father over maintenance and that Tania's friend had just found out her boyfriend was seeing a man on Facebook. She then listened as Eleanor lectured David about the importance of following his own doctor's advice and to go for tests. She also learnt about the dietary problems of Eleanor's dogs and the skin problems of Tania's labradoodle, noticing that the dog's problems aroused more interest and comment than the human ones. The walk eventually came to a natural conclusion. Everybody parted with 'see you tomorrow'.

Rachel thought about the people she had met and their relationships. The common, unifying, factor was their love of their dogs. As they walked together and watched their dogs they seemed to, almost incidentally, share very personal things. These people, who outside dog walking would not socialise, shared and supported each other in quite a special way. Rachel had never seen anything like it, but she had enjoyed their company, found it easy and relaxing.

Once they were back at the house Lottie had her breakfast and settled on a warm patch of carpet in the sunshine. Rachel did some dusting and then she sat on the sofa to do some work on her laptop. She had been toying with writing a blog about living on the Isle of Wight. The dog walking seemed a good start. She turned on the computer. Then she felt a warm head on her knees and looked down into Lottie's eyes. How could she resist?

Rachel found the dog blanket, and covered as much of the sofa as she could. Lottie jumped straight up. She tucked up close to Rachel and fell fast asleep. Rachel started writing. She, of course, would use a pseudonym.

The morning went easily, until Lottie put her head on Rachel's laptop, resulting in a long line of zzzzzzzzzzzzs. Rachel, realising it was lunch time, fetched herself a sandwich and gave Lottie a treat. Then she decided to take her out for another walk. She thought of her blog and decided that taking Lottie out was a good way to explore the Island.

Looking at the sunshine, she looked up dog-friendly beaches and took Lottie out to the car. Fortunately, it was an estate car, and Lottie could be put safely in the back. Rachel set her satnav to Brook Beach. When they arrived she found a small, but fairly crowded car park and a beach stretching in two directions. There was a smattering of people, but it was not crowded.

She let Lottie off the lead, and started to stroll calmly along the beach. To her astonishment and concern, Lottie ran straight into the sea and started swimming out towards a seagull. An older man watching his retriever jumping over the waves laughed. 'Rex loves the sea as well.' To Rachel's relief, Lottie turned around and came back to play with Rex.

While the dogs played, the man told Rachel about his wife who had depression and the worry he was having over Rex's arthritis. Eventually, the dogs stopped playing of their own accord and the man said goodbye. As Rachel walked along the beach she realised that, because of the dogs, two strangers had chatted, found out quite a lot about each other, but never exchanged names, and may well never see each other again.

She sat down on the sand and looked out to sea. It was a beautiful day. On a rock cormorants stood proudly. Above the cliffs behind her she saw a peregrine falcon. She knew that was special, but no one else seemed bothered. She looked around for Lottie and, to her horror, saw her digging frantically, sand flying in all directions. She went to see what she was doing and discovered that she had found an old ball and was trying to bury it. Her coat was completely matted with sand. Rachel called Lottie away and was grateful she followed. However, the next thing she knew, Lottie was rolling in ecstasy in a pile of seaweed. How on earth was she meant to get her clean?

Deciding that they had had enough for one day, she put Lottie on the lead and took her back to the car. She passed a few other dog walkers, who all smiled smugly at the sight of Lottie. Rachel hoped their dogs would get equally, if not more, messy.

As she put Lottie in the car she realised how unprepared she was. She had no towels or blankets, and Lottie was panting. Fortunately, she had a bottle of water, so she poured some into a ready-made hole in the car park. There was nothing she could do to save the sand and mess going into her car and, as she drove home, she was aware of a strong smell of wet dog and seaweed.

When she arrived home, Rachel took Lottie out of the car. She had started walking up the path when she heard Sarah call out. 'Hi, you look like you've had fun.'

'How am I ever going to get her clean?'

'There's dog shampoo in the bag. On a day like this you could use the hose.'

Rachel smiled weakly, then asked, 'How's Olive?'

'OK, but, you know, I think she'll end up having to go back with her daughter. Her bones are so weak. The doctor said this could happen again anytime.'

'Oh no. Do give her my love,' said Rachel, with warmth that surprised them both.

Sarah smiled. 'Of course she'll be pleased Lottie is having such a good time. She felt guilty, you know, that she wasn't doing enough for her. Lottie slept alright?'

'Next to my bed.'

'Ah, that's sweet. Right, better get on. Tinker's been looking round for a bed; reckon those kittens will be with us soon.'

Rachel took Lottie into the back garden, found the shampoo and washed her thoroughly. The little dog stood very still, although she did look miserable. When she had finished, Rachel let her run around the garden. Lottie shook and flung the water off, then rubbed against the bushes. In the bag Rachel found a brush, and, once Lottie was dry, they sat together in the sunshine while Rachel brushed her. When she had finished Lottie's coat was shining, silky smooth.

That evening, after tea, Rachel sat with Lottie, watching TV together. Rachel was wondering about Olive; she must be missing Lottie. She found her camera, took some photos, and printed them off. They weren't very good, but at least Olive could see Lottie was happy and cared for. When she took Lottie out in the garden she saw Sarah over the fence, and rushed back inside to get them.

'Could you give these to Olive?'

'Of course. What a lovely thought. I'm going in tomorrow. I'll take them.' Sarah looked down at Lottie. 'She looks very at home.'

The next morning, Rachel went back up to the castle, where she met the same group of people. The dogs greeted each other. The people started to walk

.They were half way round when they met a woman with a small black Tibetan terrier called Jazz, whom Lottie showed more interest in than any other dog they had met. The dogs walked closely by each other, often both sniffing the same clump of grass. The owner was wearing a short denim skirt and t shirt, and had tattoos on her arms. She joined the group and turned to walk with them.

Eleanor turned to Rachel. 'This is Alex. Your Lottie loves Jazz.'

Rachel gasped and wanted to run, get away, but Lottie was busy playing with Jazz.

'Nice to meet you, Rachel,' said Jazz's owner. 'I met someone yesterday afternoon. She was telling me how you were helping Olive out.' She turned to Eleanor, looking very serious.

'Tell me, have you tried that new food I told you about? It's all natural. I think your dogs will love it.'

They continued an in-depth discussion, then Eleanor turned to Rachel.

'You know, another lovely place to walk is Mottistone Down. It's gorgeous. You can let Lottie off there as long there are no cows. Sort of place you can be alone.'

'I take Jazz up there but have to watch he doesn't disappear down holes,' laughed Alex.

At this point Alex's terrier fortunately stole a ball from a passing collie. Everyone was distracted as Jazz headed off full pelt with the ball in his mouth. Rachel took the opportunity to put Lottie back on her lead, said a quick 'goodbye' and left.

Later, Rachel was sitting in the garden having lunch, when suddenly Lottie jumped up, started barking madly, and raced into the house. Rachel followed, and saw the post arriving.

Rachel picked up the letters. She recognised the handwriting on one. She felt sick; her hands started to shake. Carrying the letter into the living room, she sat on the sofa and opened it. Quietly, Lottie jumped up next to her. Rachel read the letter, crushed it in her hands and started to sob. Was there no escape? Lottie came closer and licked her face. She stayed close to as Rachel cried tears of guilt, shame and grief which she had been holding in for months. Lottie stayed by her, just being there.

Rachel stuffed the letter in her pocket and spoke to the dog. 'Come on, Lottie. Let's get out. We could try and find that Mottistone Down. I could do with being alone.'

Rachel sat in the car and set her satnav. It wasn't far.

The car park seemed quite crowded, but once through the gate Rachel saw a huge expanse of downland. She walked up the central path. Lottie ran on ahead. Even today there was a strong breeze. Rachel stopped to catch her breath. In the distance, she saw the sea sparkling, and in a field nearby a solitary house. Is that where you needed to live to get away, to feel safe? She blinked back tears, and continued on the stony path. At the top of the hill she found a bench and, out of breath, sat down. The views were stunning. Directly in front were empty harvested fields, and a small wood: layers of greens, browns and blues like a tapestry.

She heard a very noisy pipping sound coming from a blackberry bush, and saw one of her favourite birds, a long tailed tit, with a gentle pink chest, ridiculously long tail and a little round body. She put her hand in her pocket and felt the letter. What was she going to do? She thought about Eleanor and Alex. She would have to move again, but was that her life now, always moving, running away? She took the letter out of her pocket. Lottie instinctively left the clump of grass she was sniffing and jumped up next to her. As she was staring at the letter, tears running down her cheeks, she heard someone speak.

'Fancy seeing you here.'

Rachel looked up to see Eleanor. She quickly tried to wipe the tears from her face.

'Hey, what's the matter?'

Rachel shook her head.

Eleanor sat next to her. 'Tell me-'

'I can't tell anyone. I just don't know what to do.' Rachel started to cry. Eleanor sat down next to her. As if relieved of her duties, Lottie jumped down and went to join the two Labradors.

'I knew when I saw you something was wrong. It's why I told you about here,' said Eleanor gently, and then smiled. 'Not that it's actually a secret. It's special up here, though; healing, I think. See over there.' Eleanor pointed to a standing stone, not far from the solitary house Rachel had been looking at.

'That's the Long Stone. The stones over there are what remains of a six thousand year old Neolithic communal long barrow, a place for burying the dead. People probably worshipped the sun and moon there.'

Rachel frowned at Eleanor, wondering why she was telling her this.

'For me, you see,' Eleanor explained, 'it puts all my present worries in perspective. Six thousand years ago; we're just a tiny pin prick in time.'

Rachel sniffed. 'You have no idea the mess I've made of my life. You look very together, Eleanor.'

'Oh, you'd be surprised.'

'It's lovely here on the island. I don't want to leave.'

'Well don't. Tell me. I promise I won't judge.'

Exhausted, Rachel handed the letter to Eleanor.

*Dear Rachel,*

*I found your address. I had to write. I'm so sorry for everything. You didn't have to leave. We can work it out. After the initial 'stand by your man' act Jenny has told me she's leaving, so you see we can be together now. I have decided to leave politics for you. I'm going to start up my own business. Please contact me. You've changed your email and mobile. You wouldn't believe what I went through to get this address.*

*With all my love,*

*Gary'*

'So, who's Gary?'

Rachel looked down, feeling the burden of shame. 'Gary is a married man I had an affair with. I was a deputy head, respected, and he,' she glanced at Eleanor, 'He was the local MP.'

She could see Eleanor's mind whizzing, working out the puzzle. Then she saw her piece it together. 'Oh God, I remember reading about that. Are you the woman who was in the papers?'

Rachel blushed.

'I didn't recognise you. Your hair was long then, and you looked-'

Rachel grimaced. '-smart, I know. I wore makeup and suits, looked the part of an ambitious deputy head.'

'How on earth did you meet him?' asked Eleanor.

'At an education conference. I've never married. I was really happy being single, off on my mountain walking and yoga holidays. I loved teaching. Honestly, I wasn't looking for anyone. I met him, and was flattered. He said he was in the throes of a marriage break up.'

'Ah.'

'Well, anyway, we were out one night and a local journalist saw us, took photos. The story spread like a bush fire. It was last January. Maybe they wanted to write about something other than the snow. Gary had campaigned on family values. The local papers, and then the national press, just blew the whole thing up. Anyway, his wife stuck by him and I was branded a marriage wrecker. Gary said he was weak and had been led astray. I just hadn't expected the press to be everywhere like they were: outside my house, talking to my family, parents at the school gate. The school governors suggested I should take leave. It was so humiliating, but I understood why. I decided to hand in my notice. I wanted to get away. I was lucky I have savings, so I came here.'

'You were forced to leave your home, your job?'

'I'd had enough and, to be honest, I wanted a fresh start. My parents are thinking of coming over here as well. They brought me here on holiday as a child. It's wonderful.'

'So, will you find a teaching job over here?'

'That's what I'd planned. Or maybe I would have done something completely different. I love yoga. Maybe I could have trained to be an instructor.'

'So you have lots of plans?'

'Had, but is it possible to make a new start do you think? When I saw Alex I thought she might be on to it, a story, you know-'

To Rachel's surprise, Eleanor was grinning. 'Really, Rachel. It's old news. And Alex won't be interested. She's not even a proper journalist. She does the animal column, obsessed with dogs. I remember her seeing the story. She said she had no time for the man. He'd raised some ludicrous idea about people not being allowed to have more than one dog or something.'

'You think I'm safe?'

'Of course. What would the story be, anyway? 'Woman who had an affair with a divorced, unexceptional former MP moves to the Isle of Wight and walks her neighbour's dog.' Not very gripping, is it?'

Rachel laughed. It did sound ridiculous. Eleanor patted her knee.

'Honestly, don't take this personally, but no one is that interested in you.'

Rachael laughed again. 'You don't know how wonderful that is to hear.'

Lottie came running over. 'Of course, to her, now, you are very important,' said Eleanor.

Rachel stroked Lottie. 'She's been good for me, I have to say. I never thought I'd say this about a dog, but she feels like my best friend at the moment.'

Eleanor nodded. 'A best friend is someone who loves you when you forget to love yourself.' She looked over at her dogs and suddenly shouted out 'Leave!' but the dogs ignored her. 'Flipping dogs,' she said, standing up. 'Right, make sure you're up there tomorrow. Lottie needs to see her friends as well.'

That evening Rachel sat on the sofa with Lottie next to her and wrote a short, business-like letter to Gary, saying that it was over between them, and she never wanted to hear from him again. As she stuck down the envelope she caught herself smiling. It felt like the sun coming out after a long wet, grey winter. Then she heard a knock at her door. She went to answer it with Lottie close to her, and saw that it was Sarah.

'Come in' she said happily to Sarah.

They went through to the living room. Lottie jumped up to Rachel's side and she automatically started to stroke her.

'I went to see Olive. She loved the photos.'

'Oh, good.'

'The thing is, Rachel, she wondered if there was any way you would consider taking on Lottie full time. She wants to go and live with her daughter. She definitely wants to rehome Lottie. It might be that one of the other dog walkers could help, so don't feel obliged.'

Rachel looked around at what had been the sterile room. Now, there was a blanket on her sofa, some of Lottie's toys on the floor, bits of grass on the carpet. She felt Lottie's warm body cuddled next to her and stroked her soft ears. Rachel smiled at Sarah. 'I think my house just became a home.'

# Catching the Light

It was dawn on the first morning of my honeymoon. The sun was rising on a warm spring day. We were staying in a small stone cottage in a remote part of Wales. There was a long garden full of trees and shrubs. Beyond its perimeter were fields and hills. It should have been idyllic. I could hear my new husband, Steve, upstairs in the shower listening to the radio.

Steve was one of the managers at the firm in Cardiff where I was a secretary. He first asked me out six months ago. I had just come out of a very long term relationship with my school friend Mike. My engagement to Mike suited everyone; we moved in together. We were proof that opposites may attract, but could not necessarily live happily together. I was tidy; he was incredibly messy. He drank; I was teetotal. He was sociable; I was shy. All of which I could have dealt with, apart from the biggest difference, which was that I was faithful; he wasn't. This was not the fairytale I had imagined. I think our parents were more upset than us when we broke up.

I was flattered when Steve asked me out. A good looking, well off, older man. It was wonderful to go out with someone who knew how to act in good restaurants, was polite, didn't get completely legless at parties, and took me to new places like the opera and art exhibitions.

My mother was less enthusiastic. I thought it was because of the age difference.

'Erin, you're thirty. He's fifty five.'

'That's nothing, Mum. He keeps really fit, and he looks after me. Honestly, when we're out I don't have to think of anything. He decides where we go, what we'll do. He even comes with me to help me buy my clothes. He has such good taste, much classier than mine.'

'I don't want him taking you over, love. At least Mike seemed to like you for who you were. He wasn't for ever trying to change you.'

'Mike was very immature. I had to buy his underpants for him. Steve knows the right way to do things. I wouldn't want to embarrass him.'

'And what about his ex?'

'They have nothing to do with each other. They had children but he has awful trouble getting to see them. It's so unfair.'

'Well, be careful. A man that age will be set in his ways. You've all your life ahead of you. I mean, you could go travelling, anything.'

'I don't want to travel, Mum.'

'Well, what about Owen at work? He's a nice boy. When he came to give you a lift to the office meal he came in and was so friendly and chatty. Didn't he ask you out?'

I liked Owen. He was middle management, but would sit with me in his lunch breaks. He was different, into Celtic myths and legends. On weekends he went searching for holy wells. As a hobby, he was translating Welsh fairy stories into English. He was so serious about it all. I remembered teasing him, 'Don't tell me you believe in fairies?'

'Actually, they are called Tylwyth Teg or The Fair Folk.'

'And what do they look like?'

'Well, I suppose a bit like you: fair-haired, pretty eyes. You do know we both have fairy names, don't you?'

I laughed. 'I don't think there is much of a fairy about me. Last night I tripped over someone's bag in the restaurant and Steve told me I was an embarrassment. I was so clumsy.' I blushed at the memory.

Owen looked concerned. 'You went out with Steve?'

'Yes. First time last night. It was a lovely restaurant.'

'He's well off, but Erin, be careful. I've heard some funny things about him. I heard his last wife was glad to be shot of him.'

'Don't worry; he told me about her. She was very difficult to live with. She nearly bankrupted him, booking holidays, buying stuff for the house without talking to him.'

'Well, be careful.'

I turned to my mother. 'Owen is very sweet, but once Steve asked me out he seemed to just fade away.'

Not long after this conversation, in a restaurant looking over Cardiff Bay, Steve presented me with a diamond ring. I was ecstatic. I had never seen such a beautiful ring. He also told me the date of the wedding: it was my fairytale.

My real worry, though, was that my mother wasn't well off, and I knew he would want the best of everything at the wedding. I needn't have worried. Steve planned and paid for everything. Of course, it was difficult. I'd had a life time imagining my wedding. We had our first real row over it. It was over the wedding dress. Mum really wanted to buy my dress. We had planned to go shopping on the Saturday. I mentioned it to Steve.

'But I would like to buy your dress. I don't want you feeling you have to get something cheap.'

'Oh, no. Mum has money put by. Really, it'll be fine.'

'I really want to be involved; make sure the dress is right.'

'Steve, the bridegroom isn't meant to see the dress before the big day.'

'Nonsense. I have someone in mind that can make your dress. I ran a few ideas past her, actually.'

'You did what? What's it like?'

'Plain, classic empire line.'

'Like Jane Austen style?'

'Yes, very plain white silk.'

'But I had always imagined a kind of Cinderella dress; you know, like Princess Diana, but with lots of lace, and a diamond tiara.'

I saw him shudder. 'No way. That's just not going to happen.'

I felt annoyed. This was the one thing a bride was meant to choose. 'I really want this, Steve.'

'No, you are not going to be at my wedding like some Barbie doll. All my friends and relations will be there. I will not be embarrassed by you.'

His face was bright red. I had never seen him so angry. I was very upset, and started to cry, but he didn't weaken. 'You have to trust me on this, Erin. I know best.'

The next day he sent me two dozen roses. They were delivered to work. The other women were so jealous. I had calmed down: maybe he was right. And it was only a dress, after all.

The big day came. I was very nervous, petrified I would do something wrong. We had had a rehearsal the night before. Steve had been so serious, and got so angry when I messed up my vows. I thought it was nerves. Fortunately, I didn't slip, although Steve said I was too quiet. I tried so hard to enjoy my wedding day, but it was stiff and formal; there were so few people I knew. I hadn't noticed when we made out the guest lists. I didn't have much family. I had planned to ask friends from the office, but Steve said they would all get drunk and spoil it. I had my mother, but she looked lonely and on edge. Owen was also there. Steve asked him because we were using his holiday cottage for our honeymoon.

I had found a bench in the garden at the reception. I was sitting there trying to relax the fixed smile on my face when Owen appeared.

'So how's the bride?'

'Steve and I will be going soon. It was very kind of you to suggest to Steve we use your holiday cottage. We're going to go somewhere more exotic later in the year.'

'Actually, it belonged to my grandparents, but it's in a lovely place, very remote. I go there a lot. Know all the locals. There is a nice chap called Harri, at the pub. I'm sure you'll meet him, does good food. I told him to look out for you.'

'Oh that's kind. Thank you. I'm quite nervous. You know, I've never made Steve a meal. We always go out.'

'Erin, I know you don't really believe in fairies, but if you need help while you're at the cottage, look in the wooden box on the window sill.'

'You and your fairies,' I laughed.

I'm serious. You can use what's in the box to attract them.'

'Owen, I'm fine. I have Steve to look after me now.'

On cue, Steve appeared. He ignored Owen, and spoke to me. 'Come on, Erin. You must circulate.'

Steve drove us straight to the cottage, up through the winding valley roads. It was dark when we arrived. I'd forgotten how brightly the moon shone in the pitch black countryside, how many sounds you could hear: the owls, the foxes.

Inside, the cottage was rather spartan, but there was a comfortable sofa and stunning photographs of the Welsh hills. There were flagstones on the floor. The furniture was light pine, and there was a coal fire. I heard my mobile ring. Steve took it off me firmly. 'No phones here,' he joked, and put it in his pocket.

I started to prepare a meal. We were both hungry. Steve opened a bottle of wine. I was surprised. He had never had a drink with me before.

'This is very basic pasta,' I said, 'but the food at the wedding was good, wasn't it? It went well, I thought.'

'Yes, and you did well,' said Steve. He came over and held me, kissed me gently. I smiled, and wondered why I had worried.

I put the dinner on the table. He sat opposite me, and started to eat.

'OK?' I enquired.

He didn't answer.

'You do like it?'

'It's cold.'

'No, I warmed the plates.'

'It's cold,' he said, and pushed his plate away. He finished his glass of wine, and poured himself another glass, which he drank quite quickly.

'Shall we go for a walk?' he asked, standing up.

I left my food. 'Of course; it's a lovely evening.'

We walked across the field, down into the woods. Steve used the light on his iphone and guided me. Suddenly, in the bushes, I saw lights.

'Look, over there,' I said, grabbing his arm. He dropped the phone.

'You idiot' he shouted. 'You could have broken it. That was really expensive.'

'I'm sorry. I thought I saw something.'

'Don't be stupid.'

'It must be Owen, and his stories of fairies,' I joked.

'You and Owen spent a lot of time chatting, didn't you? What was he saying at the wedding?'

'Nothing. I thanked him for the cottage.'

'Bet he was wishing he was the one bringing you here.'

'Oh no, really.'

He grasped my arm hard. 'I don't expect you to be having your lunch time tete-a-tetes when we go back.'

'He doesn't mean anything-'

'I said you will stop.'

I tried to laugh. 'Anyone would think you were jealous.'

He grabbed my face. In the dark, his eyes shone. I was very scared. 'I just expect you to act like my wife. Got that?' He pushed me away, roughly.

From the corner of my eyes I saw the lights again, but brighter.

'The fairies,' I whispered.

'For God's sake.' His hand came flying through the air. It hit my face with a force that made me fall back. He turned and walked away.

My face was burning; the ground was hard: it hadn't rained for days. Stunned, I stood up and walked towards the lights, but they faded away.

I stumbled through the woods, out into the field. I didn't want to go back to the cottage, but what else could I go? Then I saw the light from the phone and realised Steve was coming back. I stood very still, but he came straight to me. 'Erin, I'm so sorry. It's been a long day. Please come back to the cottage.'

We went in together and I climbed the stairs. I washed my face, and glanced at the mirror. My right cheek was an angry red, and it stung. Steve came up. He didn't mention my face, but we went to bed.

And so I found myself downstairs on the first morning of my honeymoon, watching the dawn. I had applied a lot of makeup over the angry bruises and crept down early.

Through the window I watched the sun rise, lighting the sky miraculously with a riot of colours. So much beauty in the midst of such pain. However, this was a new day, and I resolved to make it a new start. I looked down and noticed a box on the window sill. I reached out towards it with a shaking, bruised hand, but I stopped. I could hear Steve upstairs. He would be down soon, wanting breakfast. Quickly, I put the kettle on, and set the table while he showered. Soon he was springing down the stairs. I held my breath, but he looked over and smiled broadly.

'Gosh aren't you wonderful, making breakfast for your new husband? What ever did I do to deserve you?'

I breathed a sigh of relief. Steve looked out of the window. 'Look at that weather: a perfect day.' He came over, kissed me, and we had breakfast while he told me the plans for the day. For the first time, I noticed that he did not consult me, but I quickly dismissed the thought and decided to be grateful that someone cared enough to organise a lovely day for me. We drove to the coast, and walked along the cliff tops. The views were stunning.

That evening we went back to the cottage. It had been such a lovely day. The evening before had been a bad dream.

'Shall we go to the local pub?' I suggested.

'Is it any good?'

'Owen said it is.'

Steve looked at me. I regretted mentioning Owen. But his face cleared. 'Of course.'

We went upstairs to change. I was quicker than him, and went down to get a drink of water. Then I looked over at the window sill at the box I had noticed that morning. It must be the one Owen had told me about. I heard Steve go into the bathroom upstairs. I went over and picked it up. My hands trembled as I opened it. Inside was a crystal, small and delicate. It looked like a mini cathedral. I picked it up in awe, and put it carefully in the sunshine on the window sill. It seemed to reach out and catch the light. It shimmered and glittered. I heard Steve coming down the stairs, so I quickly put it away.

It was a lovely evening for a walk. The pub was busy, the smell of food inviting. After we had eaten, a man from behind the bar came over.

'I'm Harri, a friend of Owen. He said to look out for you.'

'How lovely' I replied. 'We've had a fantastic day, and a wonderful meal.'

He smiled, but looked at my face. 'Had a fall?'

'Oh yes, I'm terribly clumsy.'

He smiled and went to get us coffee.

On the walk back to the cottage, Steve said, 'I saw you flirting with the chap behind the bar. We won't go there again.' It was nonsense, but there was no point in arguing.

When we got in, Steve opened another bottle of wine. I saw my phone on the sideboard and picked it up, wondering if my mother had sent a text. Steve came over and took it off me, laughing. 'No phones,' he said, and put it in his pocket.

I put the TV on, but we couldn't get a picture. Steve tried fiddling with various buttons on the remote, but nothing worked.

'I really want to see the golf.'

'You could ring Owen. He must know what to do.'

He frowned. 'Ring Owen?'

'Yes.'

'No, we can sort this out.'

I sat on a chair and watched as he got increasingly irritated and frustrated.

'Maybe we should phone?' I suggested quietly.

'Shut up about Owen,' Steve shouted.

I stood up and walked to the window.

'What's that, on your chair?' he demanded.

'What?'

'There: it's another remote.'

'I didn't see it.'

'You must have. You were hiding it.'

He pointed it at the TV, pressed a button, and everything cleared.

Steve rushed over to me. 'You just wanted to ring Owen, didn't you?'

'No.'

'You were seeing if you had a message from him earlier. I saw you.'

'No.'

I turned quickly. My arm caught a vase that went crashing to the floor.

'You stupid bitch,' he shouted.

I bent down to clear up the pieces. Steve grabbed my arm and threw me across the room. I hit the cold hard floor and tried to get up, but he came over, shouting at me. 'I was a fool to marry you.' Then he kicked my arms, my body, and my legs. I curled up. I was very scared, frightened he would kill me. Every part of me was in agony. Finally, he stopped, left me crying on the floor, grabbed the wine bottle and went to bed.

I lay very still for a while, then slowly got up. I crawled up on to the sofa. How had this happened? I had read about men who beat their wives, but that was other people, not me. I curled up on the sofa crying. Then I remembered the crystal. I went over to the window sill, and took it out of the box.

I didn't expect it to shine, not at night. However, the crystal seemed to reach out to the moon, catching its light, and seemed to glow. I peered out, down the long dark garden. I could swear I saw the tiny lights I had seen the night before, sparkling in the distance on the edge of the woods. Quietly, I opened the back door. I picked my way down the winding stone path and through the field.

Then I stopped. I heard music, and walked towards it. The music was gentle, seductive: plucked harps, like rain drops. I saw a circle of lights. Instinctively, I knew these were the Tylwyth Teg. I could see them clearly now: small beautiful creatures with long blond hair, dancing in a circle. Slowly, one fairy turned and looked at me. She beckoned me to join them, but I shook my head. Instead, I sat on the grass, curled up, and listened to the music. Eventually I fell asleep. When I awoke, it was dawn. The fairies had gone. It was cold and damp. I walked stiffly back to the cottage.

Of course, when he came down, Steve was sorry. It would never happen again. Each day we went out for walks, even though I was exhausted. Steve shopped in the village and we ate in the cottage every evening. Once, when I was waiting in the car for Steve to do some shopping I was startled by a knock on the window. I looked up. It was Harri. Nervously, I looked around for Steve, but he was still in the shop. Harri knocked again. I opened the door and peeped out.

'You didn't come back. Something wrong with the food?' he asked, laughing.

'No, of course not, but we've been eating in.'

'You alright?'

'Fine. Oh, there's Steve. Bye then.'

In the evenings Steve always drank. Sometimes he taunted me, made me feel small and stupid. Sometimes he hit and kicked me. It was like I had ended up in some terrible nightmare. The only escape each evening was when he fell asleep. I would creep down the garden. The music would draw me towards the fairies. Each time the same fairy, my fairy, would turn and invite me to join them. I didn't, but I would sit mesmerised by the dance and the music. At dawn, when the fairies had left, I crept back to the cottage.

Finally, the last night of our honeymoon came. We ate our evening meal in silence. I was numb with tiredness and misery. Every part of my body seemed bruised and ached. When we went to bed I lay awake as Steve snored noisily besides me. I lay on my back, very still, eyes open, too frightened to move, to think. In the early hours of the morning I crept downstairs and looked out at the darkness. Tomorrow we would be going home. What the hell was I going to do? What was I going to tell the girls in the office? I heard a creaking behind me, looked up, and saw Steve coming down the stairs.

'I'm sorry, I was just getting a drink,' I said quickly.

'I've been thinking about when we go back home.' His voice was cold.

'It'll be strange to go back,' I said. I could see Steve watching me. I felt sick with fear.

'You will not be going back to work.'

'What?'

'You're not going back to that Owen. Your place is at home now,' he sneered.

'Steve,' I pleaded. 'Please, I need to go to work. I promise I won't talk to him.'

'You must think I'm really stupid.'

I backed against the wall, but he came storming over and went to grab my arm. I managed to pull away and ran towards the fireplace. He followed and then bent to grab a brass poker. I was sure then that he wanted to kill me. Frantically, I ran to the back door, thank God it wasn't locked. I pulled it open and ran into the darkness. I could hear Steve behind, shouting and swearing, but kept running through the field and into the woods. I could hear the music and ran towards it until I reached the circle of lights. As I approached, my fairy turned and looked at me. I nodded. I would join them, I hoped for ever. It was the only way to escape. It would be the end of the torment, the hell.

I kept running towards the circle, but Steve caught up and grabbed my arm. I tried to pull away. He lifted the poker over my head. I froze. Without warning, a brilliant flash of light struck the poker. It blazed red hot. Steve screamed and dropped it. There was another blinding flash. This time it was like a streak of lightning. It shot through his body. I watched in horror as, instantly, his appearance changed. His features became wrinkled and old, his hair thin and grey. Silently, he fell to the ground.

I was aware of a feeling of warmth creeping through my body. The pain and the bruises were healing. I felt whole, strong.

I turned to the fairies. I tore off my diamond ring and tossed it into the circle. My fairy winked at me and grinned. The sky was getting lighter. It was nearly dawn. I watched as the fairies and the ring faded away.

Stunned, I stood staring at Steve, lying very still on the ground. Oh God, was he dead? Slowly, I became aware of voices behind me, then recognised the voice shouting my name. I turned, and saw Owen. He came straight to me and hugged me, holding me close. Harri was with him. He pushed past us and knelt beside Steve. He checked his pulse and phoned for an ambulance. 'He's alive. Not sure what's happened here, though.' I saw Harri looking around, mystified. I stepped back from Owen's arms and glanced up at him.

'Did Harri call you?'

'He was really worried. I came. You'll be alright now. I promise.'

Harri called over. 'Owen, take Erin back to the cottage. She looks fit to drop. I'll wait here for the ambulance.'

Together, we walked back through the woods and across the field. When we were close to the cottage I looked through the window and saw the crystal. It was bright, glistening, reaching out: catching the light of a new day.

# Belonging

*Italics are used when someone is signing. British Sign Language has been translated into Sign Supported English.*

*The word 'Deaf' with a capital D is used to indicate that a person identifies with the Deaf community and uses British Sign Language. The word deaf with lower case d is referring to deafness or a degree of hearing loss.*

Just for once it felt good not to be the one struggling. I watched the stranger. I recognised the frozen smile and intense stare as he struggled to follow the people around him signing. Out there in the hearing world I would be the one struggling, or maybe I would have given up by now and be in a corner hugging a glass of wine. I glanced over again and saw that he was slinking away from the group and making his way to the bar. He had that self conscious stoop of a very tall person. He was very fair, awkward looking. At the bar I could see that he was still unsure as he checked around nervously, trying to decide if he should sign or speak. I started to feel sorry for him, and wondered why on earth he had come to a Theatre for the Deaf.

I felt a tap on my shoulder and turned around. '*Why are you checking out that bloke?*' It was Penny.

'*Who is he?*' I asked.

'*He teaches with Ian. Apparently he wanted to see a play acted by deaf people. He's learning to sign but you can see he's rubbish.*'

'*He's good looking.*'

'*Bit nerdy. Anyway, you don't need a hearing bloke.*'

Penny walked away. I glanced back at Ian's friend. Rather embarrassingly, he caught me looking at him, so I quickly looked away. However, I was aware that he was making his way over to me, so I checked my hair in the mirrored panel on the wall.

I felt a tap on my shoulder, and turned around. I watched as he put down his pint and then self - consciously signed '*Hello.*'

I was ridiculously nervous '*Hi.*'

'*Can I buy you a drink?*' (Well, I guessed that is what he meant to sign. Actually, he said, 'Brother you drink,' but I'm used to deciphering bad signing.)

I shook my head, but signed as slowly and as clearly as I could, '*You teach with Ian?*'

He nodded. '*I am learning to sign, to help a deaf girl in my school.*'

'*Great thing to do.*'

He glanced around the room. '*It's really difficult understanding what people are saying in here.*'

'*They are using British Sign Language. It's different to your Sign Supported English; for example, we sign 'Name you what?*' I explained.

He grinned and finger-spelled 'J o h n,' adding, 'Name you what?'

'M e g a n,' I replied, slowly. I could see he was still nervous.

'I can do Sign Supported English with you.'

He smiled gratefully.

'Also, I can lip read,' I added. 'Just look at me and speak normally.'

He looked more relaxed. 'You work here?'

I nodded. He picked up his pint, took a deep gulp, then put it down.

'I liked the play; it was very moving.'

'I'm glad.'

We stood rather awkwardly. Then he looked around the room, crowded with people signing to each other.

'I've never been anywhere so crowded that's so quiet,' he said. 'Everybody here signs.'

'Of course.'

'The girl in school, she speaks and signs. She has hearing aids.'

I shrugged, and simply said, 'It's different here.'

Then some seats became free. We automatically went over, and sat together.

'What do you teach?' I asked.

He looked embarrassed. 'Music,' he signed, adding, 'Sorry.'

'Don't be sorry. I like music.'

'Really?'

'Of course. I love clubbing, dancing. Music is more than just sounds. I love the vibrations, the lyrics, the emotions.'

'Wow. Do you ever go to classical concerts?'

*'Not really; but I'd like to. What do you play?'*
*'Guitar, piano, keyboard.'*
*'How clever.'*

I noticed his body relax. He sat back in the seat, and seemed to look at me properly for the first time.

*'What do you do here?'* he asked.
*'I work on costume design and back stage.'*
*'Sorry, you do what?'*

I dug out a note pad and pen from my bag, and wrote 'costume designer'. He nodded in comprehension. From then on we used a mixture of signs, gestures and the occasional written word to converse.

*'Did you go to college or start working after GCSEs?'*

I scowled, and signed angrily. *'I got four A stars at A level. I came to university here in Cardiff to do Biomedicine.'*

He cringed. *'Sorry. Do you want to be a doctor?'*
I shrugged. *'Not now.'*
*'Why not?'*
*'I left university. I work here full time now.'*
*'What went wrong?'*

*'I could do the work.'* I said. *'Got good marks,'* I added quickly, hating that he was bound to have assumed I had found it too difficult.

He was sitting forward now, but looking at me intently, waiting. How could I explain it all to him? I was in a room full of people who would understand. Why bother trying to explain to him? He was watching me, and, I think, sensed my frustration.

*'The deaf girl in school is very bright but I always feel she is outside the group looking in. Do you understand that?'* he asked.

It was my turn to look at him properly for the first time.

I nodded. *'I went to a mainstream school as well. That girl can do the work, but that's not enough. She may be brighter than a lot of people in the class, but in the breaks she probably goes to the library, and in the evenings she goes on Facebook rather than out with friends. It's about never feeling you really belong.'*

*'Is that how you felt?'*

*'A lot of the time.'*

*'So can you speak?'*

I looked at him hard. *'I can, but I choose not to.'*

He looked very puzzled, but I didn't want to explain. Instead, I continued to sign. *'I was always on the outside and thought it was just the way it would always be. That was until I met Penny at university.'* I pointed over at her, laughing with a group of friends.

*'Did she do Biomedicine as well?'*

*'No, drama. She brought me here. It was amazing, like finding a family. Anyway, I decided to leave university, start again.'*

*'Wow, that was huge.'*

*'I suppose so, but I don't regret it.'*

*'Did your parents mind?'*

*'It was my decision.'*

I looked away, then realised the theatre was starting to empty, and Penny was coming purposefully towards me with my coat. I knew I should go, but I also wanted to keep talking to John. He was different. He wanted to listen, to understand. Mind you, it was hard going; maybe it was too much effort for him. I glanced over at him.

*'Shall we go for coffee?'* he asked.

I glanced up at Penny, who shook her head vigorously.

'*I live near here,*' John added.

I glanced over, and saw Ian looking our way. '*Is he OK?*' I asked. Ian grinned, gave me the thumbs up.

'*OK,*' I said.

Penny chucked my coat at me and left.

It was not far to John's flat, which was on the top floor of a large Victorian house overlooking Roath Park. I followed him in, and suddenly felt rather nervous away from the safety of my world in the theatre.

John fussed around, and I realised he was equally nervous. He opened a bottle of wine, poured it into two glasses, filling them to the brim so that he spilled mine when he passed it to me. Carefully, I put it down on the cluttered coffee table and sat on the edge of an old Ikea sofa. Everything in the room was shabby, apart from a beautiful mahogany upright piano that stood waiting to be played, the top covered in sheet music.

John came and sat next to me. '*I am sorry I am so bad at signing.*'

'*At least you keep trying. Most people give up.*' I smiled shyly, and moved closer to him. He leant forward and touched my hair. I pulled away. He looked at me curiously. Reluctantly, I lifted up my hair and showed him my ears. '*I hate them; they are so pointy.*'

He smiled and touched the tip of my ear. '*You are beautiful.*'

I reached out, brought down his hand, and held it. '*You have amazing hands.*'

'Pianist's hands. I was teased; friends said they were girly hands. See my wrist:, so small. I wear a woman's watch.'

We looked at each other, both knowing what the other was thinking. Who was going to make the first move? Shyly, he asked 'Can I kiss you?' I smiled, and he kissed me lightly on the lips.

I could feel my heart beating. Things were going too fast. I had sworn I would never get involved with a hearing man again: it would all get too complicated. Standing up, I said awkwardly, 'I think I'd better go.'

'I'm sorry-'

'No, it's OK. It's late.'

'I'll walk you home then. Is it far?'

The flat wasn't too far, but I was glad John was walking me home. After we said goodnight, we arranged to meet the following night.

The following night was a warm summer's evening. John picked me up. We drove down to Penarth, and walked along the cliff tops.

'I tried signing with Laura today. You know, the girl in school,' John said.

'Well done. Did it go alright?'

'I think so. She was very patient. The other kids were really interested. They didn't laugh or anything.'

'Good.'

'Last night you said you could speak-'

I took him to a bench and we sat down.

'I can talk, but I hate my voice. It's not normal. I was teased a lot about it at school.'

'That's terrible. Laura's voice is a bit flat, but actually I don't notice it now. She wears hearing aids. Did you?'

'I did. I still have some very good ones.'

He frowned. 'Then why don't you wear them? It must be better to hear properly.'

I shook my head in frustration. 'I can't hear properly, even with the best aids in the world. My cochlear is damaged, and I can only hear a few sounds. I still need to lip read and use visual cues to understand what people are saying. It is very hard work. Signing is much easier.'

'Oh, right. But you said you weren't allowed to sign. Why not?'

'Some people say that if you sign with a deaf child they won't bother to learn to speak, and then life will be very hard for them in the hearing world. That's what my Mum was told. She still won't sign with me.'

'That seems a bit mean.'

'It's complicated, but I'm glad I sign now. I feel it is my first language.'

'This is a whole world I never knew existed.'

As I saw John's face, I realised there was a whole sea of experience separating us. I forget that there are people out in the hearing world who know nothing about the world of the deaf and hard of hearing or the highly emotional arguments that surround so many issues in our world.

'There's loads more you don't know.'

He smiled and kissed me. 'You will have to teach me.'

That night I didn't go back to my flat. Neither of us wanted to say goodbye. We went out the following night and quickly slipped into a routine of seeing each other daily.

Penny, of course, was against the relationship. *'It's impossible for it to be an equal relationship,'* she said. *'People will talk to him instead of you. He will become your carer.'*

*'No. Really, it's not like that. He's different. We still sign. When we go out to eat I order for myself, and when we meet his friends he makes sure they know I have to lip read them. It's great. Honestly, he's really special.'*

It was only six weeks later that John asked me to move in with him. I knew I wanted to. Penny was furious, and not just about losing my rent.

*'It won't work,'* she said, yet again.

I thought that she was over-reacting. John and I loved each other. That was all we needed.

*'I have to get a few gadgets, like the ones at Penny's,'* I explained to John.

*'As I've never been to Penny's, I don't know what you mean,'*

*'I'm sorry. It wasn't worth taking you there. Penny doesn't understand about us. Anyway, I need to get my own stuff now.'*

*'Like what? I already know about your watch,'* he said, laughing. He had been shocked the first night I stayed to be woken up by my watch vibrating under the pillow.

*'You should see my real alarm clock: it flashes, the lot. I also have alarms for the front door and the smoke alarm. I have a TV with closed captions-'*

'*Of course. That's fine. Anything that means you'll come here.*'

After I had moved in, I realised I ought to email my new address to my mother, not that I expected her to care. However, to my surprise and horror, she invited herself to lunch the following Sunday.

'*This is going to be awful. Be prepared,*' I warned John.

'*We have to meet each other's families some time,*' was all he said. He had no idea.

Sunday came too quickly. Mum was coming over from Bristol. She arrived early. John answered the door. Mum wore her fixed determined smile. She came straight up to me, lifted up my hair, and glared at my ears. I glared back at her.

'It's lovely to meet you,' John said, not understanding what was going on, 'Would you like a drink?'

'That would be really nice; thank you,' my mother replied, with forced politeness.

I strode into the kitchen. John followed me. With a shaking hand, I tried to open the wine, but he took it from me, and put it on the worktop.

'*What's going on?*'

'*She always has to bloody check, every time. She doesn't care how I am, just if I'm wearing my hearing aids.*'

I snatched the bottle and opened it. John took the casserole in and we all sat up at the table.

I drank a lot of red wine, while John talked rather frantically to my mother. She was a teaching assistant in her local High School, so they had a lot to talk about. Mum nodded over at the piano.

'You play, John. How lovely.' She looked at me and added, 'Of course, Megan can play the violin. She got to grade seven. Quite something for a Profoundly Deaf girl.'

'*Oh God,*' I signed to John.

John, however, frowned and spoke to my mother. 'I didn't know Megan could play an instrument. I didn't think she could.'

I could feel myself getting hot and flustered. John shot me a confused look. I saw my mother purse her lips and then she said, 'Megan is very clever. She could have done anything if she'd stayed at university-'

I crashed my hand on the table.

'She could have transferred to medicine by now, you know.' My mother leant forward. She was talking straight at John. 'Instead, she's at that theatre, wasting her life.'

I stood up, walked around the table, and grabbed my mother's shoulder.

'Leave John out of this.'

Glancing at him, I realised he was staring at me as if he had seen a ghost. Of course, it was the first time he had heard my voice. Oh God, how embarrassing.

'Your voice... I can understand you.' He spoke in accusation rather than awe.

'Of course you can,' interrupted my mother. 'She doesn't need all this signing thing. She doesn't need to be in that theatre.'

I glared, too angry to speak.

My mother went very red, and looked at me. 'You had choices. Now, look, you can't even be bothered to wear your hearing aids. Do you know how hard I fought for them? They would have given you cheaper ones, but I swore you should have the best.'

'*Maybe you should wear them more,*' said John.

'Oh God,' I shouted at John. 'Don't you start. No one understands.' I burst into tears of rage, ran into the bedroom, and slammed the door.

I grabbed my cases, and started to pack. A few minutes later, John came in. He looked so cold and serious.

'Your Mum has gone.'

'*Good,*' I signed.

'I don't understand. You can talk properly and all this time you've been making me sign.'

'*I told you-*'

'Speak, don't sign,' he shouted.

'OK, you can hear me talk. Welcome to the freak show.'

He frowned. 'You sound alright, honestly-'

'No, I don't. Don't lie.'

'You were very hard on your mother.'

I burst into tears. 'Penny was right. You will never understand.'

He looked hurt, and very confused. 'I don't know what I've done wrong.'

I swallowed hard, and tried to calm down. 'I want someone who accepts me for what I am, who isn't wanting to change me. I'm tired of everything being so bloody difficult. Do you know how hard it was for me to learn to talk? Every day after school, speech therapy, wearing head-phones, and trying to hear tiny sounds, always feeling a failure. Mum, you know, she wouldn't even get subtitles for the TV. Every thing

51

was so bloody hard, and all to produce this horrible, horrible voice.'

I started to cry again, hard sobs, from years of pent up frustration.

John put his arm around me.

'I'm so sorry. But, really, you know, your voice is not that awful. Honestly, it's different, but the more I listen, the more I tune in. Really, it's OK.'

I shook my head. I didn't believe him.

'It really hurt me when you said I should wear my hearing aids.'

'But why?'

'Lots of reasons.'

I stood up, took a small box out of my drawer, and opened it.

'These are my hearing aids. These bits here are the ear moulds that go in my ear. I have always had sensitive ears. They get sore, and sometimes they get infected.'

'But isn't it worth it to hear?'

'I told you, I still don't hear like you. Imagine listening to a Mozart sonata, but take out all the high notes and then half the others. What would it sound like?'

He frowned. 'Pretty awful.'

'That is what speech sounds like to me, even with my hearing aids on.'

'I didn't realise-'

'It's OK. It's all I have ever known. You know, one day I may go back them, I may go back to talking sometimes, but this time it will be when I choose.'

He nodded and put his arm around me. '*I don't understand it all, but I'm so sorry that I have hurt you. Please stay. You belong here,*' he signed.

A few days later, I received an email from my mother, chatting about her dogs and friends, no mention of the row. I continued my work in the theatre. Occasionally I went out with John and his friends, and he would come to the theatre with me. My favourite evenings were when we stayed in, just the two of us. John even started to acknowledge that being deaf wasn't all bad. When the students in the flat below had late parties I was the one who could keep concentrating on my work, and get a decent night's sleep. He also envied the way we bonded at the theatre, and had a sense of community there which he didn't share with anyone.

However, John and I lived largely in our own little world; we were very happy. Then, one morning, I woke feeling unwell. I tried to ignore the feeling, but it went on for a few days. In the end, I went to a pharmacy and bought a testing kit. One evening, when John was out at a concert, I summoned up the courage and used it. The few minutes I had to wait seemed an eternity, but eventually I got the result I was dreading. I sat staring at the white stick, and the word I had been dreading.

Oh God, what was I going to do? No way was this planned. John and I had never talked about having children. This wasn't the right time.

I wasn't aware of John coming home. He found me sitting on the edge of the bath, and I handed him the stick. He looked very confused, and then, slowly, the truth dawned on him. 'Oh God,' he said.

'*I am pregnant.*'

'No.'

'I am pregnant.'

'Oh, my God.' His face had turned white, but then, seeing the tears on my face, he quickly put his arm around me. '*I'm sorry. It's just such a shock. Please don't cry. I'll look after you.*' He led me into the living room and to the sofa.

I continued to cry. I couldn't stop.

'*You will keep the baby, won't you?*' He looked desperate.

I nodded, but still I kept crying.

'*We'll be OK. What's the matter?*' he asked.

I realised he really hadn't thought about it. '*What if our baby is born deaf?*'

He blinked hard. '*You know I will love our baby whatever happens. Is it likely? I mean, is your kind of deafness hereditary?*'

'*They don't know why I was born deaf.*'

'*Oh, right. So we might be lucky?*'

I gasped. '*What?*'

'*I said we might be lucky and our baby-*' He stopped, and I could see him slowly realising what he had said.

'*We might be lucky and our baby won't be like me,*' I said.

'*Oh God, Megan. I didn't mean that, but obviously I want our baby to hear.*'

'*It's not obvious to me.*'

He frowned. '*What do you mean?*'

I took a deep breath. '*Why would it be so awful for our baby to be deaf? You know the community we have, and I would look after her, sign with her. She could do anything she wanted.*'

'*But you know how hard it can be as well. Anyway, what about my dreams? I want our baby to love music, maybe compose wonderful pieces, and travel the world.*'

I pushed his arm from around my shoulders, and went and sat on a dining room chair, alone. '*We both want such different things-*'

We were both motionless, silent. We were in a minefield: one false move and our relationship would be destroyed.

'I need a drink,' said John, and he left the flat. He didn't come home until late. He had never done that before. I was so unhappy. Was I being selfish wanting my baby to be like me? There was so much I wanted to give her: all the things I felt I'd missed out on. It would be so wonderful to sign with her, take her to the theatre. And she would never hear my horrible voice.

The next day, John and I communicated on a 'need to know' basis, coldly polite. It was awful. In tears, I told Penny, who suggested moving back to the flat. She said that there was a whole community that would support me. But I wanted to be with John. I knew that the thread keeping us together was fine and delicate, but I didn't want it to break.

The appointment for my first scan came. '*I'll get the time off work,*' John said.

At the hospital, we were shown into the darkened room for the ultrasound. I told the nurse I was deaf, but she kept the room dark, and, however hard John tried to keep me involved, she directed all her conversation to him. Eventually, the pictures came on to the monitor. I felt John squeeze my hand tightly, and, glancing at him, I was shocked to see that he was crying. I panicked, thinking I'd missed something.

'*What's the matter?*' There were tears slowly trickling down his cheek. I wiped them and he touched my hand.

'*Nothing. Sorry, it's just so amazing.*'

The nurse spoke to John. He signed to me.

'*Do we want to know the sex of our baby?*'

I nodded, and looked at the nurse. John asked her to look at me when she spoke.

'You are having a baby girl,' the nurse said.

I glanced at John.

'*Perfect,*' he signed, and we smiled at each other for the first time in weeks.

I hadn't seen my mother since that terrible Sunday lunch, but after the scan I knew it was time to tell her. I was dreading seeing a look of disapproval, of that awful feeling that I'd messed up again.

We arranged to meet outside a small café. I arrived early: my mother was always prompt. While I was standing outside the café waiting, a woman pushed past behind me. I stumbled forward. My hands went straight to my stomach, and I glared back at the woman, who quickly apologised. I couldn't smile back. I felt so angry with her. I felt she might have hurt my baby. At that moment my mother arrived.

I saw her gaze go straight to the side of my head. Her hand moved, but she didn't touch me. We sat down.

After exchanging a few polite remarks, I finally told her I was pregnant. She sat very still. I waited for a lecture. However, her eyes filled with tears.

'You're going to be a mother?' she said.

I nodded. 'You're going to be a grandmother.'

'Oh Megan, that's wonderful.' She burst into tears.

I was shocked. I couldn't ever remember seeing mother cry. I looked around self-consciously in the café, but no one was looking at us.

Mum wiped her nose in a business like way. 'I'm sorry. It's a shock. My little girl is to be a mother.' She took a long swig of coffee. 'How are you? How's John?'

'Alright. I've stopped being sick, which is great. We had our first scan.' I pulled out the photograph and noticed her hands were shaking as she held it.

'It's a little girl.'

She gazed at the photograph. I touched her hand and she looked up. 'Mum, what do you think the chances are that she will be born deaf?'

She shrugged. 'I've no idea. No one knows why you were born deaf. You know, I always worried I'd done something wrong, but they said I hadn't.'

'You felt guilty?'

'At first, but then I just got caught up in the battle of trying to prove you were deaf.'

'You mean you knew before them?'

'Oh yes. Mothers often do, you know. Wait till you have your baby. You get a sort of instinct. It took two years before they believed me.'

'But you kept fighting?'

'Of course. Later, when the professionals told me it was important for you to have good hearing aids, to learn to talk, that is what I focussed on. I didn't want you to miss out on anything. You were bright, and I didn't see why you shouldn't do anything you wanted.'

'I can understand that, but, Mum, it was hard. I was very lonely sometimes.'

She fiddled with the wedding ring she still wore. 'I know. Maybe I should have let you go to the School for the Deaf, but, you see, you'd have had to board, and I couldn't bear the thought of it.'

'I don't think I'd have liked sleeping away.'

'I don't think you would have either. I wouldn't let them send you.'

'I'm glad I didn't go. So you fought them on your own?'

'I did. They said that the boarding school was for bright deaf children. They said it was the only way you'd achieve your potential.'

'So it meant a lot to you that I did so well at school?'

'Of course. Getting into university, well, it was like a miracle.'

I looked out of the window, at the people walking past, chatting, all caught up in their own worlds.

Mum fiddled with her ring. 'Look, I don't understand you leaving university, but I've been thinking. You're my only daughter, and I don't like us not speaking.'

'The signing, Mum. It's not about you: it's about me.'

'I suppose so. I don't understand that either, but at least I gave you a choice, didn't I?'

'Yes, Mum, you did that.' I took a deep breath. 'Mum, if my baby is deaf I shall sign with her. In fact, even if she is hearing, I will. I do appreciate what you did for me, but this is what I want for her. I know you did what you thought was right for me, but this is my choice.'

Mum put her head to one side. She was choosing her words carefully. 'OK. I will respect that.'

I could see how hard she was trying, and so I added, 'And maybe, one day, I'll go back to wearing my hearing aids. Not yet, but I promise to think about it.'

'Thank you, and I promise to try and break a habit of a lifetime, and stop checking you are wearing them.'

We both reached across the table and touched hands.

John and I went to antenatal classes. I was lucky in having a really good teacher and a great midwife, both taking time to speak to me and explain things. I started to trust her, and even spoke to her sometimes. I was given plenty of handouts as well, so I could read things up at home and ask questions when I saw them.

I decorated the spare room. I had seen the latest baby books with black and white pictures, but I wanted my baby's room to be full of colour. However, I left one wall plain. One day she would tell me what she wanted on there.

I was in the flat on my own on the due date. The contractions started gradually, but, as they got stronger, I became frightened. I sent a text to John at school, and was so relieved when he came home.

'*I'm so scared,*' I said.

'*Me too,*' he replied. We held each other close.

I went into the hospital at ten in the evening. Midwives and doctors kept coming in and out. John told me what they were saying. Eventually, at five in the morning, our baby was born. I was exhausted, but elated. We'd chosen her name: Anwen, Welsh for beautiful. John gazed at her adoringly and touched her ears. '*Little pixie ears like her Mum.*' Neither of us dared say anything.

When we went back to the ward, her cot was put next to my bed. I had brought in a special alarm so that I would know when she was crying. However, nothing seemed to work properly, so I decided that I would wear my hearing aids. John brought them in for me.

'*I will use them,*' I said, '*but I'm not speaking any more than I have to.*' He saw me turn to Anwen, who was crying. 'Wow, you can hear our baby.'

'*I can hear her in my way, yes,*' I said, and lifted her into my arms.

Anwen may have been tiny, but she filled our world. She was jaundiced. We had to stay in hospital. John was on paternity leave and stayed in as much as he could, but it was difficult when he wasn't around. Most of the nurses assumed I could hear normally because I was wearing hearing aids. There were all sorts of problems. I couldn't understand them when they spoke to me at the same time as filling in charts, or turned away. I had to speak. Some seemed to understand easily but others just didn't have the patience. I kept a notebook and pen by my bed. Fortunately, my midwife came on to the ward armed with leaflets and tried to help.

Having not worn hearing aids for a long time, the environmental noises of trolleys crashing and people shouting was stressful, and there were times I longed for my quiet world.

My mother came in that evening. She held Anwen close, in awe, like us, of our little miracle. She simply glowed with pride. She looked at me, then blinked. I knew she had noticed my hearing aids. She went to speak, but stopped herself. Instead, she pulled something out of her bag and handed it to me. It was a baby's book, and, when I turned it over, I saw that it was a nursery rhyme with signs. It had cost her a lot more than money. 'Thank you,' I said. She smiled, but went back to watching Anwen, fast asleep in her crib.

As she left, John arrived. It was late. He went straight to Anwen, then looked at me. He signed, '*You know her hearing test is tomorrow?*'

'*Of course.*'

It was a long night. I was up most of it with Anwen. I saw dawn break from the hospital window. I had just settled Anwen after a feed when she started to cry again. Exhausted, I got out of bed and leant over. For once, it was quiet on the ward. Nervously, I decided to speak as well as sign. 'Hush, lovely.' Instantly, her crying got quieter. I spoke and signed to her again. 'Hush now.' I saw her relax and settle. Suddenly, there was a terrible racket in the corridor, the sound of a shrill alarm. Anwen's eyes shot open, and she started to cry.

'False alarm,' a nurse called.

'Shush, darling,' I spoke, and signed again. I watched her slowly relax and go back to sleep.

Then I knew, as certainly as my mother knew that I couldn't hear, that my daughter could. I sat up, stunned, glad I had found out on my own. I needed time to think about it, without John, without my mother around. My daughter could hear. She was not deaf. Eventually, I spoke and signed to my baby, 'Anwen, you aren't deaf, not like your Mummy. My voice is different to some people, but you stopped crying when you heard it, so I think you must like it, and that is all that matters to me.' I looked down her at her tiny ears and her tiny fingers. 'Maybe you'll have Daddy's fingers, maybe not. I think maybe you'll just be Anwen, and, actually, that's just fine.'

It was then that I realised I didn't want to change anything about her. Anwen opened her eyes and stared at me with those intense, sapphire blue eyes. I signed and spoke. 'You will hear things I never have. I hope my voice doesn't embarrass you. You'll hear Daddy's voice and his wonderful piano playing. But you will also sign and I'll take you to the theatre and Deaf club, and you'll be part of a wonderful community as well.'

John came in, and we took Anwen for her hearing test. I didn't tell John what I believed; maybe I was wrong.

Finally, the doctor gave us the result. 'Her hearing seems fine, but obviously we'll have to keep checking.' John collapsed on to the seat. Then he looked up at me nervously and signed, 'Are *you OK?*'

I smiled, signed and said, *'Fine, you?'*

*'Yes, but if she was to become deaf for any reason, I know I'll be fine with that as well. We'll still sign with her, all the time, what ever,'* he said.

*'Of course,'* I replied, but gently.

I looked down at Anwen, signed and said, 'Welcome to our world.'

# The Outing

Kay heard John slam the front door and drive away in his BMW. Silence. Checking her watch, she rushed into the bedroom. Rummaging under the bed, she found a tightly wrapped carrier bag and put it in the packed holdall which she had hidden at the bottom of her wardrobe. Once downstairs, she rushed around, checked everything, and grabbed her jacket. She glanced up at the twenty year old photograph of John standing in front of the foundations of the first Evans' Spa Hotel, sited here in the Welsh valleys. They lived in the largest house in Blenwyn, John's parent's home town, and it was in this town he directed his philanthropic work. He had become the town's reference point, the 'Godfather of Blenwyn'. There was also a smaller photograph of her with John collecting his MBE last year. It was not a good photo of her. She looked ghost-like: fair hair, grey suit and fascinator, and her eyes were closed. However, it was a very flattering picture of John, transformed from the chubby, nerdy chap with a beard. He stood proudly in a designer suit, with stubble and body to match.

As she opened the front door she noticed things written on the special pad John had bought her, 'Kay's to do list'. She tore it quickly, folded it, and put it in her pocket. She felt guilty that she was not going to be here ticking off the list, guilty that she was going away without telling John, guilty about what she was going to do. However, the chains of guilt which shackled her were not strong enough to hold her today.

Determinedly, Kay walked down the driveway, past her old Skoda, and out into the street, joining an untidy straggle of people, all heading down the steep street lemming-like towards the train station for the commute to Cardiff.

Glancing up into the distance, she took her daily sip of comfort from the distant hills. They had been the stunning backdrop to her life, every day different but the same, today blue-green, shimmering in the early morning heat. She was thankful it was good weather; it would make a difference later. On the pavement opposite, Megan, the papergirl, was pushing her bike. She shouted out to Kay, 'Morning Mrs Evans. I just saw Mr Evans going off. What you up to then?'

'Llenwyn' she said quickly, glad she had prepared a story.

'Oh. Why's that then?'

'I thought I'd try the new gym there.'

Kay could see Megan had further questions, but she walked on quickly down the high street, past a row of terraced houses which opened straight on to the pavement. There was number six where she had grown up with her Nan, never dreaming she would be living in the 'posh house' one day. The next door neighbour's front door opened, and a woman in an apron picked up her milk.

'Morning, Kay. You off to catch the train, then?'

'That's right. I'm going to Llenwyn.'

'You not driving?'

'Thought I'd take the train for a change.'

'Oh right. You going to that new gym?'

'That's right.'

Kay walked on, thinking that celebrities who moaned about intrusion should try living in a small Welsh town.

Further down the street she noticed a smart single-storey building, 'The John Evans Community Hall', and then a sign to the 'John Evans Playing Fields'. It was as if her husband had played monopoly with the town and now owned the board. At the bottom of the hill she found her eyes drawn to a building site previously occupied by the enormous Welsh chapel her Nan had attended. Now, it had been demolished and they were laying the foundation for John's next dream. Kay secretly, deep down, was uncomfortable that John should be planning to take over the town's former place of worship.

She arrived at the tiny station, which had two platforms, no waiting room or buffet, nowhere to buy a ticket. Most commuters were cocooned in their own world, listening to ipods, reading papers, and texting, but a few were chatting. One woman standing next to Kay lifted her face to the sun and said in awe, 'It's so warm, so dry!' Kay agreed. In a place where rain and drizzle were the norm, she reckoned a certain amount of sun worship was excusable. Kay's phone signalled a text from John: 'Chase up architects (see emails). Don't forget drinks on Friday approx 20.' 'OK,' she replied.

The train arrived. Kay got in, and sat down, keeping the holdall on her lap, her arms wrapped around it protectively. She leant back and closed her eyes, always tired, always feeling one step removed from her life.

Suddenly, a strong, confident, challenging voice asked, 'OK if I sit here?' Kay opened her eyes and recognised the tall, attractive woman with very short dyed red hair and smart linen shift dress.

'Rhiannon, of course. It's lovely to see you.' This was not true. It was actually rather awkward. Rhiannon's husband, Alun, was a major shareholder in John's business, and Rhiannon had managed some of the hotels. Although they were essentially John's friends, they had socialised together as couples, occasionally going out for meals and to the theatre down in Cardiff. However, a few months ago, something, and Kay was not sure what, had broken the relationship. John had announced that Rhiannon had given in her notice. They would not be seeing them socially anymore. He would give no explanation, but was obviously upset. Kay had wondered what was wrong but felt it would be disloyal somehow to contact them.

'Where are you off to?' Rhiannon asked.

Kay didn't reply: her phone signalled another text. 'Make that 30 for drinks. We'll need decent food.'

Kay sighed. This was obviously something to do with raising backers for the chapel project, invites to rich and influential backers. John's notion of decent food would involve her spending hours making canapés.

'OK,' she replied again, and mumbled, 'More bloody canapés.'

She glanced up, noticed Rhiannon looking at her, and tried to laugh. 'Sorry, but I swear I'll be expected to produce a thousand assorted canapés to get into heaven one day.'

'You have a reputation for your catering. I couldn't be bothered. Get caterers in.'

'John likes to make a point that we have put the effort in, not just hired caterers, and I really want to support him. This project for the chapel is going to need a lot of investment.'

'What's the latest on that?'

'It's expanding all the time. It's still basically going to be an arts centre, a theatre, restaurant, exhibitions and that kind of thing, but now there is some talk of a casino as well. I'm not so comfortable with that, but John says it's essential for getting the investment.'

'A casino in Blenwyn?'

'He thinks it would be great for the town, provide jobs.'

Rhiannon raised one eyebrow. 'And call it 'The John Evans Centre'. Yes, I could see that.'

Kay heard the bitterness in her voice. 'He does a lot for the town. He's a good man.'

'Almost saint-like.'

Kay felt rather annoyed. 'Because of him Blenwyn is a really thriving valley town.'

'He's not done too badly out of it either, has he?'

'He deserves it.'

'Alun has some big reservations about this latest project-'

'I don't ask about the business side. I just try to support John.'

Kay looked out of the window, and saw they had been leaving Blenwyn.

'John said you'd resigned?'

'That's right.'

Kay glanced at Rhiannon, and saw the tightly pressed lips.

'We should go out again sometime. You know, as a four.'

Rhiannon frowned. 'You don't know about me and Alun?'

'Sorry?'

'We split up a few months ago.'

'Oh, John never said.'

'He never said anything? Didn't tell you why it happened?' Rhiannon sounded incredulous.

'Nothing.' Kay didn't understand. What was she meant to know? 'Anyway, how is Sam coping?'

'He's fine, four in August. He spends most weekends with Alun down in his flat in Cardiff, and then the week with me. Alun is taking him away for a few days soon. He's such a good dad, but then he was a good husband.'

Kay could hear sadness rather than bitterness in Rhiannon's voice. Kay really liked Alun. If anything, she found him easier to get on with than Rhiannon. He had a gentler, more forgiving way.

'Sam is such a darling. You know, if you ever need a baby sitter. It doesn't take long for me to drive out to your house.'

'Thanks. Actually, Sam really likes you. You're good with children.'

Kay looked away, but was waiting. Any minute now would come the question people knew they shouldn't ask but couldn't resist.

'You never wanted a family?'

The question never got any easier to answer. 'We decided years ago. It was for the best. Now, of course, it's too late.'

Kay noticed Rhiannon's frown, but fortunately she didn't ask any more about it.

The guard came along. 'Open return to Cardiff, please,' requested Kay. She caught a quizzical glance from Rhiannon, who showed a season ticket.

'You're staying away, then?' asked Rhiannon.

'Just a night.'

'John will have to look after himself?'

'He's away. He went off this morning.'

'Oh, right. Where's he off to this time?'

Kay shrugged, looked down. 'I don't know. He goes away a lot on business. He'll be back in a few days, definitely by Friday.'

'You really have no idea where he's going?'

Kay felt interrogated. 'No, it's not important. We have mobiles. I can contact him if I need to.'

'It's a bit of a novelty you going off like this, isn't it? I mean, you usually stay at home.'

Kay's phone rang. It was John.

'You in the gym?' he asked.

'On my way.'

'Well, don't take long. I don't know why you're going; you've never bothered before.'

'I just thought it would be good for me. I thought you'd approve.'

'Not when we're so busy. As soon as you get back, contact the architects.'

'You need the revised quotes?'

He tutted irritably. 'I told you. I need them for Friday. I've got some really big prospective investors coming. Make sure it's a good spread; also decent wine: these people know their drink.'

'Of course. I'll get it sorted.'

'Good, all you need is in 'Main Chapel File'. There are so many people to chase up. Did you find the 'to do' list?'

'Yes, thanks.' Then she remembered what Rhiannon had said. 'Where are you?'

He paused. 'Oh, just travelling, you know. I'll be in touch again tomorrow. I'll be really busy, so just text or email me any queries. Right, better go.'

Kay put her phone away.

'Mobiles are great, aren't they?' commented Rhiannon.

'Mm.'

'Well, John could be anywhere, and, of course, so could you.' Their eyes met.

'What work do you do now?" asked Kay.

'I'm self employed, buying and selling online; antiques mainly. My father owned an old fashioned antiques shop in Abergavenny. I learnt a lot from him. It's good fun, and flexible.'

'So, do you go to auctions and things?'

'Sometimes.'

'What happens at them? I mean, when you go in, what do you do?'

'Why the interest?'

'Oh, nothing.'

'What?' said Rhiannon, laughing.

Kay bit her lip. 'It's a secret really.'

'Oh, go on. Tell me.'

It would be good to tell someone. Kay pulled out a printed leaflet. 'Please don't tell anyone, but I'm going there.' She spoke defiantly.

'Really?' enthused Rhiannon.

'I've never been to an auction before. I'm very nervous.'

'Are you aiming to buy anything in particular?'

'Yes. It's, well, it's embarrassing, but it's just something I have to do.'

'This is very intriguing,' smiled Rhiannon. 'What is it?'

Kay shook her head. 'I'd rather not talk about it.'

Rhiannon picked up the leaflet. 'I know them well. Reputable auction house.'

'Oh, good. I was worried. I don't know anything about this sort of thing.'

'Why are you going on your own? I hate to admit it, but John would be good at this kind of thing.'

'No.' Kay realised she spoke too harshly. 'I mean, I want to do this on my own. It's personal. John wouldn't understand.'

Rhiannon sat back, and put her head to one side. 'There's more to you than meets the eye, isn't there? How will you get there?'

'I Googled it. It should be a twenty minute taxi ride. It starts at eleven. I'll have time to look around first.'

'Sounds interesting. You know, I wouldn't mind coming along.'

Kay panicked.

'You don't mind, do you?' asked Rhiannon.

'But surely you have plans for your day?'

'Nope, this was a day for me. Mum has Sam for the day and the night, so I'm a free agent. I was going to traipse around shops all day, hence the flats.' Rhiannon held out an elegant foot in delicate sandals very different to Kay's own Birkenstocks.

Kay was feeling trapped. She couldn't think of a reasonable excuse to put Rhiannon off going with her. 'I don't know-'

'Look,' said Rhiannon, 'I can see this is a bit delicate, but, honestly, I'll just be there if you need me. Mostly, I'd just like to have a look around for myself.'

Kay, not used to being assertive, could feel herself relenting. In some ways it would be less stressful to go with someone who knew what they were doing. 'Thank you. That would be great.'

They sat back, both glad of time to themselves. However, soon they were approaching Cardiff.

Looking out of the window, Kay was struck again by what a chaotic, raucous and cosmopolitan city Cardiff had become. Once they had alighted form the train she felt carried along by the crowds on the station. She held nervously to the stair rail as they made their way down the steep concrete steps. Outside the station, she glanced over and saw the top of the Millennium Stadium in the distance, a symbol of change. Rhiannon was more than equal to the place, and went straight to get a taxi.

Kay became increasingly nervous on the journey. She couldn't talk anymore. She just sat, trying to breathe, her hands sweating. She was shocked when they arrived at an industrial estate. She had expected a grand old Victorian house. Rhiannon, however, didn't seem surprised.

They went in and Rhiannon showed Kay where to get her bidder's card.

'Need a catalogue?' Rhiannon asked.

'I've downloaded one,' said Kay, pleased she didn't look completely disorganised.

They walked around, Rhiannon excitedly pointing out interesting things, but Kay was single-minded. Then, in the distance on a wall she saw a number of paintings. She saw the one she had come for instantly and hurried over. There were four paintings by her artist, three in expensive frames. The one she wanted, though, was in a cheaper plain frame which she guessed had been bought ready-made. The picture was alive, vibrant, terrifying. She walked cautiously towards it. She reached out her hand. She lightly touched the side as if testing to see if it would burn her. Her hands shook; her throat hurt; there were no tears.

Rhiannon came over, looked at her concerned, and asked, 'Are you alright?'

Kay nodded.

'Sure? You've gone awfully pale.' Rhiannon looked more closely at the painting.

'This is what I've come to buy.'

'It's good. You know the artist?'

Kay just nodded. She felt very sick.

'Do you want to go on in? You look in need of a sit down.'

As they sat, Rhiannon perused the catalogue.

'The estimate for your painting is twelve hundred pounds. Of course, it could go for more. Then there's the buyer's premium. That's another twenty percent.'

'I know.'

'Well, if this is a surprise for John, he's very lucky.'

'It's not for John.'

'Oh.'

'I looked up to see if I could pay in cash. It said I could. That is right, isn't it?'

'Cash?'

Kay picked up her holdall, and glanced around furtively. She unzipped it, opened the plastic bag, and whispered, 'I've two thousand five hundred pounds.'

Rhiannon eyes widened. 'Bloody hell, Kay. Why on earth aren't you paying with your card?'

Kay said seriously, 'I don't want John to know about it. It's not his money. I sold some old jewellery.'

'What ever are you doing?'

Fortunately, at that moment, the bidding started. Kay was distracted for a short time watching people bid, some in person, others by phone. The auctioneer was more relaxed than she expected, and generally the lots went through swiftly. Most people knew what they wanted and what they were prepared to spend. Then she heard the name 'Mark Cape'. The auctioneer explained in detached tones that the artist had recently died, that his work was increasingly sought after, and that they were very fortunate to have four of his paintings on sale today. The larger paintings in the expensive frames were first and went for more money than Kay could afford. She started to feel nervous. Maybe this was going to be completely beyond her reach? Lot 36 was announced. A white-gloved woman held it up. Kay blushed. God, it was terrible watching everyone looking at this painting coldly, as if it was any old object to be bought and sold.

'Lot 36, acrylic by Mark Cape (1948-2010) entitled "Nude on the Beach." Fourteen by twelve, signed and dated lower right. You'll see the estimate is twelve hundred pounds. This is a delightful picture, set on the Gower Peninsula. This is a previously unknown work from the artist's personal collection, never exhibited before. We will start the bidding at five hundred pounds.'

'Thank you. I have six hundred, seven hundred, eight hundred, nine hundred, nine-fifty, one thousand, eleven hundred, twelve hundred-'

Kay sat panicking. It was going so fast. She hadn't bid at all.

'Now, do I hear thirteen hundred pounds?'

Kay raised her paddle. The auctioneer nodded.

'Fourteen hundred. Do I hear fifteen hundred?' He nodded at Kay. She held her breath as the auctioneer said, 'And do I hear sixteen hundred? No?' He looked around. 'Any increase on fifteen hundred?'

Finally the hammer went down. The painting was hers for one thousand five hundred pounds.

Kay sat still, and suddenly felt very calm. It was hers; she had it. She wanted to cry, but bit her lip hard. Rhiannon said she was happy to go, so they went to the cashier. Kay counted the wads of notes on to the counter.

The painting was wrapped. Kay picked it up. It was lighter than she expected, and easy to carry. They ordered a taxi, and went outside to wait. The fresh warm air hit her face, but still she felt in a trance. They waited for the taxi in silence, and then travelled back to Cardiff station. Once they had got out of the taxi Kay turned to Rhiannon.

'Thank you for coming with me. It was a big help.'

'I enjoyed it. So are you finally going to tell me what this is all about?' Rhiannon gestured towards the painting.

Kay shook her head. 'I can't, and, please, don't say anything to anyone.'

'But where will you hang it?'

'I'm taking it somewhere. That's where I'm going next.'

'Where's that then?'

'I need to get straight on another train. I'm going to Swansea,' Kay said.

'Swansea?'

'Yes, actually to the beach where it was painted.' Kay spoke firmly.

'A kind of pilgrimage?'

'Sort of.'

'It all sound very romantic.'

Kay cringed at the word.

'So, are you meeting the person in the painting or someone to do with the artist?'

'No, I'm going alone.'

Suddenly, Kay felt overwhelmed with exhaustion. She had planned this for so long, but still there was the most difficult part to do.

'This is very important to you, isn't it? Are you alright?'

'I'm fine.'

'So you plan to go to this beach?' Rhiannon looked at her watch. 'What time do you think you'll get there?'

'About six. Luckily, I have enough money for taxis from Swansea to Gower, where the beach is. I checked. It will be about fifty pounds each way I reckon, but it will save time.'

'You're very well organised. I think you should be working for me,' said Rhiannon, laughing. 'So will you come back to stay in Cardiff tonight?'

'Maybe, or Swansea. I'm not sure how things will go.'

Kay saw Rhiannon weighing something up. Please God, she thought, don't ask.

'I quite fancy coming.'

'Oh, no-'

'Really, I think I'd like to.'

'No. I've mucked up your day enough.'

'We can split the cost of the taxis.'

'I've enough money.'

Rhiannon looked serious. 'I can see you want to go on your own, but there are things I need to tell you, and I've a feeling this beach might be the right place to do it.'

'I don't know-'

'Please-'

Rhiannon's' voice was gentle and kind. She already knew so much. What was the harm in her coming?

'It's a clamber to the beach. Your dress and shoes aren't suitable.'

'My problem,' said Rhiannon briskly.

'I don't know-'

'Go on. Really, I've nothing to do, and I'm intrigued now. I want to see where the painting was done. Come on, these things are better with company.'

'Well I suppose-'

'Good. Let's get going. But first, there's something we really have to do.'

Before she could argue, Kay found herself dragged into the Marks and Spencer food hall on the station. Rhiannon grabbed a basket, and filled it with sandwiches, crisps, chocolate and drinks.

'I'm starving. We need to keep our strength up.'

Kay managed to smile.

They had a ten minute wait for the train and the journey was about an hour and a half. Outside Swansea station they found a taxi willing to take them to Gower.

'It'll cost, mind you,' the driver said.

'I know,' said Kay.

'Right then, let's get going.'

The taxi driver was very chatty but, fortunately, Rhiannon kept the conversation going. The driver drove them along the seafront, and then up inland. Kay could feel her stomach muscles clenching. This was the way he'd driven her. It looked too familiar. Oh God, what was she doing?

The taxi stopped at the edge of the village.

'You girls want to go straight to the beach then?' The taxi driver sounded sceptical and Kay could understand why. They didn't look like walkers or backpackers.

'This is fine, thank you.'

'Right. Well, at least it's a nice evening for you.'

They got out. It really was beautiful. Kay felt sad that she couldn't just enjoy the breathtaking beauty of the place. She had forgotten just how special it was. They started on the path down to the beach. The painting was awkward to carry, but Rhiannon helped with her bags. Fortunately it wasn't too far, and they were soon at the secluded sandy cove.

'Wow,' said Rhiannon. 'This is gorgeous.' She took her sandals off. 'The sand is so warm.'

The tide was a fair way out. Kay took off her sandals, and felt the sand work its way between her toes. For a moment she remembered her childhood visits to the beach at Barry: happy innocent times.

There was only one family there, and they were packing up. Kay and Rhiannon sat and had a drink. Rhiannon took some photographs on her phone. Kay watched as the family left the beach. The little boy looked back at the sandcastle he had obviously spent hours building.

Kay knew that she could not put it off any longer. She unwrapped the painting. It was a picture of this beach, late on a summer's evening. Along the water's edge, a naked woman stood with her back to the beach. Her arms were outstretched, her head flung back, her eyes closed, her blond hair hanging down. She remembered standing there in a trance-like state.

Rhiannon took the painting from her, looked at it properly for the first time, and gasped.

'My God. Is that you?'

Kay snatched the painting back.

'How did you meet this Marc Cape?'

'He was like a guest teacher at the life drawing class I went to.'

'So, when was it painted?' asked Rhiannon.

'About fifteen years ago.' Kay blushed.

'You were married then?'

Kay nodded. 'About three years.'

'I see. Did John know about any of this?'

Kay shook her head. She turned the painting over, relieved it was such a simple frame. She began to remove the painting.

'What are you doing?' asked Rhiannon. 'Don't take it out here. Sand and water will ruin it.'

'Look, Rhiannon I have to do something. You won't understand, but I need you to leave me alone. Stay here, OK?'

'OK.'

Kay picked up the painting, and began to walk down to the sea. There was a breeze that cooled her face. She had imagined this moment for so long. She was very excited.

She reached the water's edge. The sun was resting on the horizon. She felt the warmth on her face. Slowly, she walked into the sea. It felt cold. The water slowly covered her feet, her ankles, her calves. It reached her crop trousers, but she didn't care. Suddenly she was aware of Rhiannon running down the beach.

'Kay, stop!' shouted Rhiannon. 'Come back.'

Kay ignored her. She went in deeper, then leant forward and held the painting under the surface. It seemed to struggle to come back up, but she held it there, drowning it. At first the painting appeared unaffected, but slowly the paint started to run; the paper became heavy, soggy.

Rhiannon had reached the water's edge. 'Kay,' she screamed.

Kay stood up straight in the water, holding the ruined painting. It had gone. She had finally destroyed it. She watched the sun slipping below the horizon. She had done it, and it was destroyed. She had imagined at this point running jubilantly out of the sea. However, her wet clothes dragged her down, and the paper was heavier and more awkward to carry.

'What the hell?' asked Rhiannon. Kay ignored her, walked back to their things, found the bin liner she had brought and stuffed the painting in it. Then she changed into the dry clothes she had brought, and sat down, staring in front of her.

'My God. You just paid fifteen hundred pounds for that picture,' said Rhiannon.

'I had to destroy it, get rid of it.'

'Why?'

'For years now I've felt guilty, ashamed of what happened. I thought if it was gone I would be free.'

'And are you?'

Slowly, Kay shook her head. No point in pretending: nothing had changed.

Rhiannon looked very serious now.

'Tell me, Kay. Tell me about the painting.'

Kay sat down. Blackness was starting to streak across the blue sky.

'I was doing these classes. Marc came. He was so complimentary about my work, and about me. I fell for all the smooth words and let Marc persuade me to come here and have my picture painted.'

'Did it seem romantic?'

Kay nodded. 'Not really romantic, but here I felt I was someone completely different. Free, beautiful, young... I can't believe I did it now, but it was how Marc made me feel. It was like it was the most natural thing in the world to take my clothes off here-' She glanced at Rhiannon, adding with a faint smile, 'There wasn't anyone here, you know. We came a few times.'

'And one thing led to another?'

'Well, no. Marc said we mustn't sleep together. He said all the passion must be in the painting. Anyway, one evening he shouted, 'It's finished.' I hadn't seen it before then. I remember coming running up to him.'

'What did you think?'

'I was shocked. The innocence I had imagined was completely absent. It was so sensual, and intrusive. I felt like he had stolen part of me. Then he said 'It's time,' and I knew what he meant.'

'What happened?' Rhiannon whispered.

Kay hugged herself. She closed her eyes.

'He pulled me towards him, and kissed me. I'd imagined the moment, you know, so many times. It would be warm, and I'd be floating -'

'And-'

'I felt nothing. I pulled away, and I told him to leave me alone. He looked hurt, but said, 'At least I've finished the painting'. Kay's head fell and her body started to shake. Quiet tears turned into sobs. She screamed in pain as the pent up emotion of years forced its way out. Rhiannon put her arms around her and held her. Slowly, Kay calmed and continued her story.

'I remember standing there, screaming, 'Give me my painting; you must give it to me.''

'No way,' he said. 'It's really good. Don't worry. I'll never sell it. This way I shall always have a piece of you.'

'I felt such shame at what I had done. I'd been unfaithful to John, and that painting would always be there as a reminder of my guilt.'

'What happened?'

'Marc just took me home. I never told John, but just vowed to be the best wife I could. I watched out for the painting to be on sale but it never was. Then Marc died, and his family wanted the money; hence the auction.'

'Oh, Kay,' gasped Rhiannon.

'You must think I'm awful. I should never have let him paint me.'

'Were you happy when you met Marc? Happy with John?'

Kay clenched her fists. 'I know it sounds terrible, but I was lonely. John was always away, but even when he was home he didn't seem to notice me. We had separate bedrooms so he could sleep. He was always tired. I wondered about children but he said we had to wait.'

'It sounds pretty grim.'

Kay looked directly at Rhiannon. 'No, I was being selfish. John was such a catch. I'd had a very sheltered life being brought up in that tiny terraced house by my Nan. To be honest, I think John wished he'd married somebody brighter, prettier. I was lucky he stayed with me. Thank God he never found out about Marc. He's a good man, so loyal. I'm so lucky.'

Rhiannon leant forward. 'Kay, I have a feeling you have allowed guilt from Marc to totally blind you to the reality of your relationship with John.'

'Oh no. It's all my fault really.'

Rhiannon took her arm away from Kay. Her face turned stern and hard. 'OK, I think it's time to put a few things straight about John.'

Kay blinked. 'I know you don't like him-'

'I didn't resign for business reasons,' interrupted Rhiannon.

Kay drew a deep breath. 'Oh God, no. You can't mean you and John?' she said faintly.

Rhiannon shook her head. 'Not me and John.'

Kay frowned. 'I don't understand.'

As Kay and Rhiannon sat on the beach, Alun was pouring two glasses of wine. He passed one to John. As John looked up, he gave Alun that gorgeous smile. He felt a momentary thrill. Then he stopped himself. Enough.

'So, what's so urgent that we need to talk about?' John asked lazily.

'A few things.' Alun took a deep breath. 'Firstly, I am selling my shares in the business. I'm pulling out.'

He saw John put his head to one side, smile. 'You don't mean that.'

'I do. I've threatened to do it a few times, but this time I mean it. I've turned a blind eye in the past. Some of the people you are getting involved with are downright criminal. I don't want any part of it.'

'Oh, come on.'

'No, really, John. You could end up in prison. I want out. I am going to work for Helen Davies in the bay.'

'What? She runs that charity housing association doesn't she?'

'That's right, something I believe in, something I can proudly talk about to Sam.'

'Oh God. What about when Sam wants a new mobile, designer trainers?'

'We'll sort it out, and talking of Sam, there's something else.'

There was no smile now. He could see John getting angry.

'What?'

'Me and you, it's over. God knows why I've let it go on so long.'

'I was the one to support you when you came out. Because of me you were able to move into this flat.'

'I know what you did, but enough. I know you've been seeing other people.'

'They don't mean anything to me.'

'No, but I'm not sure anyone does. I think to be honest the only person who matters to you is John Evans.'

'I do so much for that town; give Kay a better home than she could ever have dreamed of.'

'But Kay, poor Kay. You don't give her anything that matters. Time, love, honesty.'

'Kay is alright. She's one of those women who love just to look after other people. Don't worry about her. She's fine. This all suits her. Without me, she'd have nothing. No one else has ever wanted her, have they?'

Alun stared. What had he ever seen in this man? 'I'd like you to go now.'

'You don't mean it. Come on, you need this relationship as much as me.'

'You've always told me that, but finally I can see it's not true. Please go.'

'You don't mean it.'

'I do. Go now, and never, ever, come back.'

John stood up, furious. 'Fine, have it your own way. You'll come grovelling back.'

'Never. And for God's sake, be honest with Kay.'

'No way. She doesn't notice anything. She sleep-walks through life.'

Alun felt sick. 'And that suits you?'

'Certainly does,' replied John.

'And what about Kay?'

'What about her?'

Finally, Alun saw the real man. The mask finally melted away. Before him stood a self-centred, selfish man who saw nobody's needs but his own.

'John, you need to learn grown up emotions of empathy, caring and love. I'm not the person to teach you. Now go.'

John shrugged and left.

Kay sat on the beach in the fading light. She and Rhiannon had cried and talked for hours. Despite all the denial and heartache she slowly became reconciled to what Rhiannon was telling her. Pieces of a thousand piece jigsaw were slowly put together. She sat up straight, saw the final parts of the sandcastle being washed away, wondering if the little boy would be back the next day to build a new one.

Kay picked up the jacket that was lying on the sand. From the pocket she took out 'Kay's To Do List'. She realised that she had torn off an additional blank sheet by mistake. Taking John's list, she determinedly tore it into tiny pieces, and pushed them into the bin liner with the ruined painting. Despite the darkening sky, she could see clearly. She knew now there were no chains: she was free.

# Free to Be Tegan

*What follows is an extract from the novel "Free to Be Tegan" which was published in March 2015. It is available for Kindle ereaders from all the Amazon websites and is also available as a paperback book from Amazon.*

# Chapter One

'You have chosen the path of darkness.'

Tegan stood on the wooden stage in front of the Community, determinedly staring at the digital clock at the back of the room. 0730. She waited for the dull click. The numbers flipped. 0731.

In the cold, bare meeting room, a shaft of light from the London spring morning crept in through one of the high windows.

'You have been weighed in the balance and found wanting' continued Daniel. He stood to her right, at the other end of the stage, his hard voice echoing off the peeling cream emulsion walls. She didn't dare look at him. The room was silent. Tegan, unblinking, waited. 0732.

'You have chosen the sinful pleasures of the Domain of the Beast. You have grievously sinned against The High One and this Community. You refuse to repent, to curse and reject all that is of the world.' She heard him pause. Even now he was waiting, seeing if she would break. Tegan stood expressionless, very still, apart from the slight rise and fall of her shallow breaths and the secret grinding of her right thumb into the palm of her left hand. Her shapeless clothes hung off her: a calf length dark brown skirt; plain beige blouse; bulky blue acrylic cardigan and large black headscarf, tied at the nape of her neck. The community uniform. Silence. Her eyes crept down from the clock to the tops of the bowed heads of the women at the back of the room. Along the row she saw her mother, Sarah, her hands clasped tight on her lap. She glanced forward and accidentally met her father's gaze, a look that said that this failure was inevitable. She slowly turned her head to her right. Daniel stood, neat white hair and beard, and long loose white shirt intricately embroidered with gold thread, the earthly personification of the High One. She heard his voice, louder, more passionate.

'Tegan Williams, you are commanded to leave this Community. From this time forth you are dead to us, to your earthly parents and the elect. You will be judged with all those in the Domain of the Beast. On the day of judgment the High One will show you no mercy and you, Tegan Williams, will be thrown into the lake of fire, there to suffer for all eternity.'

Her breathing quickened, the grinding into the palm of her hand grew harder. She felt him willing her to look at him. She could not resist. Slowly, she turned her head and met the gaze of the man whose teachings she had followed, the man she had revered and worshipped. His eyes were narrow, eyebrows down and his mouth was tight. His anger was like a volcano waiting to erupt, waiting to burn and consume her.

Then, clenching his fists, he turned, descended the steps and stood with his back to her. The elders in the front row stood and turned their backs to her also, and then the rest of the Community silently stood up and started to turn away. Tegan's eyes darted to her mother, who was turning slowly, stiffly, around. A sharp lightning pain shot through her. This was really happening. This was their final judgment, the end.

Tegan staggered down the steps and left the room alone. The dark hallway was deathly quiet. She climbed the hard wooden steps, brushing past the cold, white, sterile walls. She had been five years old when the Community had moved into this derelict Victorian hospital. She remembered how enormous, empty and dark it had seemed and how she had excitedly run through the huge echoing rooms. It remained sparsely furnished throughout her early years, but the severity of their lives had taken a new turn with the arrival of Daniel. So much had changed then.

She entered her bedroom, the room she had slept in for twenty two years. The room now had white, bare walls apart from a lurid picture called "The four beasts". She knew every detail: the lion with eagle wings; the bear with ribs between its teeth; the four-headed leopard with wings, and the beast with iron teeth and ten horns. They were set in a blood red sky above a stormy sea: all seemed to snarl out of the picture at her. Above it a digital clock showed the time, a constant reminder of the approach of the end of the world.

There were two beds in the room. For years she had shared the room with Esther, who had been her only close friend. Four years ago Daniel had declared Esther was to marry and now Esther's role was to support her husband and their two children. Martha, a critical, pious girl had been given Esther's bed. Tegan had little in common with her but at least someone was there if she woke at night: anything was better than waking up alone. She wondered idly who her bed would be given to next. Tegan turned around quickly, stood on tiptoes, and pulled down a battered suitcase from on top of the wardrobe. It should have been empty, but when she undid the catches she found a large brown envelope inside. She recognised her mother's handwriting, and frowned. Her mother had obviously put this in here secretly. They had not been allowed to communicate for weeks. Maybe these were her final words of dismissal. She couldn't bear to read them, not now. She quickly stuffed the envelope into her plastic shoulder bag. Then she started to take her clothes off the wire coat hangers and fold them carefully: more plain skirts, blouses, acrylic cardigans and black headscarves were placed in the suitcase. Next, her spare pair of brown lace up shoes, grey underwear, light tan tights and two cotton nightdresses. From her bedside table she took her alarm clock. It was a yellow, old-fashioned wind-up clock with a loud tick. Next to this lay a well thumbed copy of "The Revelations of Daniel, The Omniscient."

She stroked it, kissed it, and placed it gently in her case. With it she placed the framed verse "He Shall Come like a Thief in the Night". She opened the drawer. She carefully took out a small piece of embroidered material, touched it lightly and packed it. Finally, she reached to the back of the drawer and found a small rectangular silver box with engraving in the top. She took it out, checked the contents, clutched it, and then wrapped it carefully in one of the skirts in her case. She took a deep breath, left her room and walked down the hall to the bathroom. It was a large white tiled room, a row of basins one side, cubicles the other, no mirrors. She found her toothbrush and returned to her room.

Tegan was just doing up the catches of her case when the door burst open. She saw Daniel and, behind him, her parents. 'Tegan, you have filled your parents with shame. They have the right to have the final word.'

Tegan was breathing fast. She dug her fingers deep into the palm of her hand. Daniel gestured to Philip. He shuffled forward with hunched shoulders. He pushed back the round metal glasses with his forefinger and then pointed at her.

'Tegan, you have always been a proud, rebellious child.' His voice was flat, but underlying was the tone of perpetual disappointment he used when speaking to her. 'Your mother and I have spent many hours in vigil for your soul but to no avail. To think we have come to this, for you to blaspheme against our leader Daniel, to doubt and question him in that most proud and sinful way. From this moment we, your parents, with the whole community, disown you.'

Tegan turned to her mother for some drop of mercy. But the look of cold dismissal she saw was even harder to bear than any words.

Philip continued, 'On the Day of Judgment you will be judged more harshly than the world for you were shown the light and have rejected it.' Philip spat out the cruel words. He could have gone on like this for hours but somehow the words from him seemed hollow. She heard an ambulance screaming outside: any minute now she would be cast out into the world to join the damned.

Philip sneered, his finger jabbing in her face. 'You have chosen a wicked, dark place. The animals of the world will tear you apart and feed you to the dogs and in that we rejoice.' He stopped.

Daniel stepped forward and, as if comforting a grieving relative, put his hand on Philip's shoulder. He bent his head, mumbled a prayer in a different language, and they all turned and left the room.

The room was silent. Tegan looked down at the palm of her left hand, dry, cracked, red raw, bleeding, but she felt nothing. She found an old piece of tissue in her bag and with a shaking hand tried to wipe it clean.

Finally, from out of the wardrobe she took a shapeless beige rain coat, put it on and buttoned it up. She picked up her shabby plastic shoulder bag and suitcase, opened the door, and, without glancing back, left the room.

She walked down the stairs and glanced at the clock that hung over the front door. 0750. Next to this

94

was a huge white board. Every day Daniel wrote the date and a verse for them to meditate on, and the date. Today it read March 1st 2006 and underneath that the verse for the day:

*"Depart from me, you cursed, into the eternal fire prepared for the Beast and all those in his domain."* She guessed Daniel had chosen that for her. She could hear familiar quiet droning prayers of vigil being said in the meeting room. 'Come Quickly Oh High One'. The whole Community including the children would repeat it over and over again for an hour. Every day had started like that for her for twenty two years, but not today. For the first time in her life she was an outsider.

Tegan opened the front door out into the cold drizzly rain and descended the flight of concrete steps. She was hit by a wall of noise: the early morning rush hour. Alone she walked across the concrete forecourt and opened the iron gates. She saw a taxi driver swearing at another driver, a parent shouting to their children to hurry up. The rain added to the sense of urgency as the world rushed about its business. She glanced down at the bins on the pavement and, blinking hard, realised she had been put out with the rubbish.

# Chapter Two

Despite the rain Tegan staggered across the road to the park and through the familiar wrought iron gates. This was her secret sanctuary, a place she would occasionally visit for a few, precious moments of privacy. She found a wet metal bench, put down her bags and perched on the edge. In an effort to calm her mind she made herself focus on her surroundings. The blossom on the trees above her was still in tight bud, but the daffodils strutted proudly, defying the dreary morning. Commuters clasping umbrellas and briefcases, parents with pushchairs, dog walkers being pulled by their dogs: all hurried past. A group of teenagers proudly underdressed in dripping wet navy school sweatshirts were shouting over their plugged-in iPods. Then she noticed in a quiet corner a woman standing with a toddler, holding the child's upright arms. The little girl, wearing bright pink wellingtons, was splashing in the puddle and giggling. They were in their own blissful world.

Tegan looked over at the Community house and realised for the first time that no one would be missing her. She had ceased to exist to them. She swallowed hard, looked away. Defiantly she picked up her bags and stiffly stood up, aware that the rain had soaked through the back and shoulders of her thin coat. It was time to go.

Tegan left the park, walked quickly down the High Street, past chain stores and cafes, down side streets, past boarded-up shops, small grocers', and sari and charity shops. Her eyes scanned the shop fronts: he had said he lived above a shop, a Spar. There it was. Yes, there was his name on the metal intercom, "Steve Crocker". She hesitated, feeling sick with anticipation. He had no idea she was coming, but he had told her to do this, hadn't he? He had said that she needed to "find herself", be more independent. The last time they had talked, he had touched her arm, kissed her on the cheek. She shivered at the memory. Of course he would be able to help her, tell her what to do.

She took a deep breath, and pressed the intercom. 'OK' a disembodied voice answered. She clenched her teeth with anticipation at the sound of his voice, and heard the door release. Tentatively, she pushed it and went inside. The hallway was grey concrete. She started to climb the stone steps. She could see a front door open on the landing, hear the radio blaring "Soldiers' wives have asked for a meeting with Tony Blair."

As she neared the top she heard Steve shout 'One day you'll remember your bloody keys.'

Puzzled, she approached the open door, and stood in the doorway. She could see Steve sitting at an old wooden table, a mug in his right hand, the other holding open a book lying flat on the table. There were books and old newspapers strewn everywhere, a tatty sofa; on the walls framed maps and a poster for a production of Hamlet. Steve glanced over casually but, on seeing her, clumsily put his drink down, spilling it over his book.

'Tegan. My God.'

'I'm sorry.' Tegan stammered and looked away, deeply embarrassed.

She watched him register her embarrassment, then realised he was only in his boxers.

'God, sorry,' he said, and rushed into the bedroom.

She heard him stumbling around as he shouted 'Come in.'

Her stomach twisted with embarrassment. She stayed in the doorway.

Steve came back into the room wearing a crumpled checked shirt and doing up his jeans. Still she blushed, aware of the intimacy of the situation. She hadn't imagined it like this.

'Come in,' he repeated impatiently.

Tegan took one step forward. He took off his red-framed glasses and, with the other hand, rubbed his forehead, ran his hand over his close shaved head.

'So what - I mean, how? God, Tegan, why are you here?'

'I've been cast out. I've left the Community.'

'What?'

'It's complicated, but I've been told to leave. It was awful - but you said it would be good to get away, didn't you?'

'In theory,' he said evasively, 'but you said it would be very difficult.'

'I know it's a big thing, but I thought you'd be pleased.' Tegan searched his face but there was no reassuring smile.

'But what will you do?'

'I don't know. I thought you would tell me.'

'Why did you think that?' he asked. Then he looked perplexed. 'How did you know where I live?'

'You mentioned the Spar.'

'Right-'

'I thought you'd be pleased,' she repeated. He didn't reply. She put down her bags.

'I know I haven't any money but I can get a job. Of course, I wouldn't want to move in-' Her voice was getting more desperate. 'You said it was the right thing to do. We can be together now.'

She heard the downstairs door open, and saw Steve's eyes dart to the front door, which was still ajar. The look of consternation on his face was turning to panic. A female voice called breathlessly.

'Sorry it took so long. I had to wait for the croissants. Still they are really hot.' Steve stepped forward just as a woman appeared in the doorway. In an abandoned gesture she kicked the door fully open and flung open her brown fake fur coat proclaiming 'Just like me!'

Tegan stared in horror as the woman revealed skimpy scarlet underwear. What kind of world had she come into? The woman, however, seemed unabashed.

'Shit! Didn't know we had company,' she said, glancing at Tegan and laughing.

Steve turned to Tegan and spoke in harsh tones she had never heard before. 'This is Alice. She is my fiancée.' It was brutal.

Tegan blushed and looked down. She dug her nails in to her hands.

'Alice and I are getting married.' Steve enunciated the words as if he was speaking to a child.

'I'm sorry,' she stammered, still not daring to look up. 'I didn't realise-'

The room was spinning. Steve's words were echoing far away. Tegan grabbed hold of the back of the chair. She swallowed hard, and then forced herself to look at Steve. Their eyes met.

'You are getting married?'

He nodded.

'But what about us?' she asked quietly.

'There is no us Tegan, there never was.'

Tegan glanced at Alice, who had pulled her coat together, and was walking towards Steve.

'Who is this?' There was no anger, just total bewilderment in Alice's voice.

'This is Tegan. I met her a few times at the library.' He smiled at Alice. 'There's nothing going on.'

'Well, obviously,' Alice grinned, 'but why is she here?'

As Steve and Alice both turned and looked at her, Tegan remembered the time she had found an enormous toad in the garden. Captivated by the beautifully ugly creature she had looked at it in the same way they were looking at her.

'She's in a bit of bother, says she has left this religious group she's been living with, you know, the group who live in that big old building by the park.'

'Oh God, well, would you like a coffee or something?' asked Alice, obviously not sure what to do with Tegan. She reached forward and touched Tegan's arm. 'Shit, you're drenched. Hang on. I'll get you some dry things. Have some croissant or something.'

Tegan shot a look at Steve, but she saw an infinitesimal shake of his head: his eyes were pleading with her. She couldn't ignore the fact that he was desperate for her to go.

'No, no thank you,' Tegan said, as she started to pick up her bags and walk to the door.

'You will go back to them won't you?' said Steve.

She couldn't answer. Steve came and stood between her and the door. 'Go back. You must, you know that.'

She pushed past him, stumbled down the stone steps and out into the street.

Steve went to the window and watched Tegan walking away. From up here she looked even more fragile and vulnerable. Swamped by that long shapeless brown coat and enormous headscarf, she walked in flat brown shoes like a clumsy school child.

'Poor girl,' remarked Alice. 'Has she got learning problems or something?'

'Actually, she's bright. She's just led this very strange life.'

'She obviously had feelings for you.'

'Rubbish.' Steve looked away, hiding a spasm of guilt.

'Steve, she wouldn't come here for nothing. You said she came to the library. There must have been more to it than that?'

'We did go for coffee. I was interested. Her life in the community is fascinating, and I'd never met anyone like her.'

'And how did she know where you lived?'

'Apparently I mentioned the shop. I don't remember that. Mostly she told me about her life in the community.'

'So you found her interesting, a novelty?'

'No, not just that. I felt sorry for her,' insisted Steve.

'Did you say you'd help her?'

Steve squirmed. 'No, of course not. I may have suggested that she should leave the community-'

'And that she could come to you?'

'No, No. For God's sake, Alice. I never said that, it was nothing. I never thought she'd leave. Look, enough of the interrogation, she'll be alright. Come on, let's have some breakfast.'

Down below, Tegan was staggering blindly down the High Street. What had she done? People impatiently pushed past her. She stepped off the pavement.

'Move, you stupid cow -' shouted a driver over his horn. Tegan got back on the pavement and went and sat on a seat in the nearest bus stop. Pigeons pecked close to her feet, looking for crumbs among the cigarette butts. She pulled her feet back. She hated birds. They were always waiting to peck and scratch you. She wanted to curl up and die. Tears poured down her cheeks. She felt so ashamed at how she had behaved, what she had seen. To have loved someone like that. She had trusted a heathen man. She had ignored all the warnings.

*"No pure thing can exist in the Domain of the Beast."* Steve had deceived her. She had thought he was a good man and that he would tell her what to do.

The rain grew heavier. What was she going to do? She sat chewing hard on the quick of her thumb. She was hunched up, rocking slightly. Dreams of proving to the Community, to her mother, that she could come out here in the world and live a pure, good life were crumbling. She was alone: no money, no food, no friends, nor anywhere to stay. *"A valley means a wrong turn."* That's what they said. This was all her fault.

What was she going to do? Daniel knew her heart; he would never let her back in the Community. She stared at the traffic. Then she remembered the envelope from her mother. She pulled it out of her bag, and opened it, numbly. It contained a letter and two envelopes. She took out the letter. It was written on a scruffy piece of lined paper.

'Tegan, I am writing this without permission. For this I shall pay penance. You have chosen the world over your own family, rejected those who have loved and cared for you all your life. I fear for your soul. This is the last thing I shall do for you as your earthly mother. You must resist the temptation to live in sin with this heathen man. On the back I have written the address of my sister, Aunt Hannah, and her husband, Uncle Ellis, and their phone number. Contact them. I believe they will give you shelter. Be warned. These relations are not of the elect. Trust no one. You will need what is in the larger envelope. I am ashamed of it. I am glad to get rid of it. Despite the terrible hurt and suffering you have wilfully inflicted on us I will do vigil for your soul. Yours in Him, Your Mother.'

Tegan stopped reading. Despite the harshness of the words, this letter must have been very difficult for her mother to write. Her mother must still care. She turned over the page, glanced at the address and grimaced. That was ridiculous, how on earth did her mother expect her to get there? She replaced the letter. Full of curiosity, she pulled out the thicker envelope. It had the name "Sarah" written on it in fountain pen. It was held together by an elastic band. She took this off and put her hand inside. Frowning, she started to extract the contents. As they were revealed, her eyes widened, her hands started to shake. Alert, she glanced around at the people around her. Had anyone else seen? She quickly shoved the contents back in, re-tied it with the elastic band, and returned it to the envelope. Quickly, she replaced the whole lot back in her shoulder bag, zipped it up, and squashed it tightly under her arm protectively. What on earth was she going to do?

# Chapter Three

'Bloody Daffodil' muttered Ellis Davies, trying to pin the drooping flower on his jumper: St David's Day again and a hectic day ahead. But he was excited: so much work had gone into this concert. Of course, it was a far cry from the professional concerts of his life before retirement, but the thrill was still there. He stood in the music room of the Georgian Manor he had moved into with his wife Hannah on his retirement five years before. He looked out of the long patio windows, and mentally shut out the sounds of the builders above with their radio. Out there were his Cambrian Mountains. Over thousands of years they had remained miraculously unchanged. Today the distant hills were blue green, traces of the remnants of ice and snow on the highest peaks. He saw a red kite, enormous flashed wings, soaring high in the sky. His face relaxed. Further down the valley was a small cottage, "Hafan", his childhood home. That was his reference point. He still went down to the cottage to work sometimes, and revelled in its remoteness. Of course, the manor was a beautiful old building. He could understand why Hannah had wanted to live here. Also, the farmhouse on the land was perfect for his daughter Cerys. He had been pleased she had her own place. Tucked away in the garden, it was perfect for her. But, for all that, his heart was down there in that tiny cottage.

'You struggling with that daff?'

He turned to Ruth. Petite with short brown hair, Ruth was the wife of the village publican. She idolised Ellis, choosing to imagine a far greater level of fame and prestige than he had ever actually attained. He knew she found his appreciation of her work organising the choir and concerts deeply flattering. The bulk of his fortune had actually been made, not from solos in great opera houses, but in the royalties received from his chance involvement in music for some major films. However, he did nothing to dispel the myth, and Ellis, for his part, thoroughly enjoyed this more glamorous version of himself.

Ruth put down the programmes she was carrying. 'God, Ellis, the poor thing is completely mangled.'

Ruth plucked a fresh daffodil from a vase and broke the stem. Even though he was broad rather than tall, she had to stand on tip toes to pin it on his jumper. Her hands were shaking but she pinned it perfectly.

'What would I do without you?' he asked.

Her dark brown eyes shone with pleasure. 'You know Martin has dropped out? Well, I was thinking, why don't you do it, you know, sing "Maffanwy"? People would love to hear you: it would be the highlight of the concert.'

He smiled, but shook his head. 'No, I won't sing, not in this concert. You know that I never do it on principle. It's about discovering new talent. Actually, I have given the solo to James.' He spoke the words with

106

an air of martyrdom. It seemed a long time now since he'd enjoyed the applause of an audience and he missed it more than he cared to admit.

He picked up the programmes for the concert. The layout was not particularly inspired but the contents were accurate. He saw Ruth watching him anxiously, waiting.

'Marvellous.' She beamed in response.

'I hope we fill this concert hall, it's so much bigger than any other place we've used.'

'Oh we will, thanks to you. When I think how amateurish we used to be before you came. You know, already three quarters of the tickets have been sold.'

'Fantastic. Let's hope the rest go as well.' He heard the house phone ring and grumbled, 'Not more last minute changes.' He picked it up.

'Yes?'

'It's Sarah.'

'Sarah?' He was trying frantically to remember who she was and what was she doing in the concert.

'Yes. Sarah, Philip's wife.'

He gripped the phone, his mind erasing any connection with the concert. 'Duw' he said, sitting down, his hand shaking. He started to scratch at his greying beard, coughed, and cleared his throat. 'I didn't recognise your voice. It must be more than twenty years. How are you all?'

'It's Tegan,' Sarah said.

'What's happened?'

'She rebelled, Ellis. She's been cast out.'

Ellis was aware of Ruth standing close by, looking at him curiously. 'Coffee?' he mouthed in a bid to get rid of her. She nodded obligingly and left the room.

'Sorry Sarah, what do you mean?' he asked, trying to speak more slowly, more reasonably. However the answer did nothing to assist him.

'She's been shunned by the Community, put out into the Domain of the Beast,' came Sarah's reply.

'Sarah, what the hell are you talking about?'

He heard Sarah tut irritably. 'She has been made to leave here.'

'Let me get this straight. She has been living with you and Philip in the Community but now she has been thrown out?' He spoke as one translating a foreign language.

'That's right. She refuses to repent, to curse the world and the works of the evil one.'

Ellis couldn't believe this was the Sarah he used to know. She had always been serious, but now she sounded so intolerant.

'It all sounds very traumatic,' he said, 'but she must be twenty seven or so now. I guess she'll go and live with friends, get a flat or something?'

'The only person she knows in the world is this man who worked in the library. I pray she will resist the temptation to live in sin with him.'

'But what do you expect her to do? Has she friends from work who can help?'

'We have kept her pure from the world. She has never been to school or worked in the world.'

'I didn't realise.' He felt overwhelmed. 'So I assume you and Philip will be leaving as well. Do you want to come here?'

'Philip and I will not be leaving. We will have no more to do with Tegan.'

'Duw, you can't mean you are not going to look after her?' He was stunned. How could Sarah act in such a callous way?

'We have taken care of her all her life, but now she has shown she neither respects nor appreciates anything that has been done for her.'

'I'm sure that's not true, but in any case you can't abandon her to the streets of London. You can't just disown your own daughter. How do you expect her to cope? How much money does she have?'

'She has some cash, no bank account of course.'

Ellis took a deep breath. Exasperated and shocked, he said 'It sounds to me that her only realistic option is to go to this man then.'

'I have urged her to resist a life of sin. Actually, there is another option. I have suggested that she contacts you.'

'Contacts me?'

'You do see that you and Hannah must provide her with shelter, don't you?'

'You can't possibly expect Hannah to help after the way you've behaved.'

'That was different. I have told Tegan to come to her aunt and uncle. I have provided her with enough money to travel to you.'

'But it would be so difficult and, in any case, she doesn't know us from Adam.'

'Ellis, it is your duty to help.'

'Oh Duw.' He could see there was to be no reasoning with Sarah. 'You say she has money. Does she know how to get here?'

'She has your number. She must contact you and sort that out.'

'I think you'd better give me her mobile number,' said Ellis reluctantly.

'She is not allowed to own a mobile phone.'

'Bloody Hell, Sarah. She's so vulnerable. Anything could happen to her.'

'She has chosen to rebel. She must bear the consequences. She is very fortunate I am helping her at all. I really shouldn't be doing this,' said Sarah, her voice tight.

'So she will have to find a phone box then. Hope she can find one that works. Otherwise, what will she do?'

'She must find her own way now.'

'Aren't you at all worried about her safety?' he asked desperately.

'From this time forth she is dead to us.'

'Sarah, that is a terrible thing to say,' he said quietly. She didn't reply. He sighed and said, 'So I just have to wait and hope she gets in touch.'

'I have done what I can. Listen Ellis, Philip must never know I have phoned. Don't contact us. I shouldn't have used his phone. I'd get into terrible trouble if he found out.' The voice that had been so stern sounded like it was verging on hysterics.

'You don't even want me to tell you she's safe?'

'No, I want nothing more to do with her. And there is one more thing Ellis-'

'What?'

'If she does come to you, you must keep your promise, you must say nothing. Tegan knows nothing. You mustn't tell her.'

110

'Of course, you know you can trust me Sarah.'

'I don't trust anyone in the world. I will go now. I can do no more.'

With that she had gone. He sat shell-shocked. How could the Sarah he had known speak, behave, like this? She'd had a wonderful singing voice but there had been no hint of beauty or music in her voice today. He guessed life married to Philip would be pretty tough. A hard, fanatically religious man, Philip had the gift of crushing any hint of joy out of life. What had life been like for Tegan? He guessed she would go to this boyfriend. Sounded like she'd finally had enough of the community place, wanted to make her own life. How prepared was she though? He couldn't help being worried about her. What if she didn't phone? It was terrible to feel so helpless.

Ruth came back into the room carrying coffee.

'Hope you put something in that' he said.

'What's happened?'

'That was Hannah's sister, Sarah. Hasn't spoken to us for years. Apparently her daughter is in some kind of bother. She was asking me to help if the girl contacts me.'

Just then he received a text. He took a deep breath.

'What now?' asked Ruth.

He sighed with relief. 'It's only Hannah wishing me luck.'

'I'm surprised she remembered. I mean, she's busy enjoying New York isn't she?'

'I guess so. Actually, maybe it's as well she's away at the moment. Anyway, come on. Let's get on with the concert, eh?'

111

In London Tegan thought about the money. *"Mammon will burn your soul."* Five hundred pounds! It was sinful to even handle this amount of money. Her mother would never steal, but how on earth would she have got hold of this amount of money? It was extraordinary that she should have such a sum. Tegan started to walk aimlessly down the street. She saw a young girl lying in an old sleeping bag in a doorway.

*"A valley means a wrong turn"* she heard again. What had that girl done? What sin was in her life to lead to this? Tegan looked at the girl: cold, alone. People skirted round her, looked the other way, and treated her like some unpleasant mess on the pavement to be avoided. She would not end up like that girl. She was stronger than that. But what would she do? Could she live out here, away from the Community, stay pure? People pushed past her. The rain got heavier. She had to find shelter. She started to walk down the street, and saw a large, rather squalid, Bed and Breakfast with vacancies. She swallowed hard. Could she really go in there on her own? Would she be safe? She thought about these people in Wales. Maybe it would be safer with them at least for a few days, but how would she get there? Why on earth did her mother suggest people so far away? She was getting very wet and tired. What was she going to do?

*I hope you have enjoyed these first three chapters of "Free to Be Tegan". To read on, please go to Amazon to download the Kindle version or to buy the paperback.*

_http://www.amazon.co.uk/Free-Be-Tegan-cult-herself-ebook/dp/B00UC9R1YM_

_http://www.amazon.com/Free-Be-Tegan-cult-herself-ebook/dp/B00UC9R1YM_

# About the Author

I was born in Cardiff and have retained a deep love for my Welsh roots. I worked as a nursery teacher in London and later taught Deaf children in Croydon and Hastings.

I now live on the beautiful Isle of Wight with my husband, where I walk my cocker spaniel Pepper and write. I have two grown up children.

'Catching the Light' follows 'Free to Be Tegan,' my debut novel. My second novel, due for release later in 2016, will be set on the spectacular Gower Peninsula.

Thank you for reading 'Catching the Light'. If you have enjoyed it please take the time to post a short review. It really makes a difference in encouraging others to have a look at it. Thanks. And contact me at marygrand90@yahoo.co.uk if you would like to be notified when my next book is released.

Mary Grand

61234296R00067

Made in the USA
Charleston, SC
17 September 2016